DISCOVERED REDEMPTION

DISCOVERED REDEMPTION

JULIE BAWDEN DAVIS

Roses
ARE
RED
PUBLISHING

Cover by Judy Bullard (customebookcovers.com)

Book design by Julie Bawden-Davis

Palm logo design by Kayla Curry

Roses are Red logo design by Kyle Kane

This is a work of fiction. Characters and incidents are the product of the author's imagination. Any perceived likenesses are coincidental.

ISBN-13: 978-1-955265-33-1

ISBN-10: 1-955265-33-X

Distributed by Roses Are Red Publishing

rosesareredpublishing.com

❀ Created with Vellum

ACKNOWLEDGMENTS

As they say, it takes a village. Here's my village. I'm supremely grateful to each of these fabulous people!

ARC Reading Gems
Julie Schlueter
Tara Bradley
Heather Wamboldt
Kery Bailey
Susa Fraccaroli
Trish Darrenkamp
Marilyn Smith
Lisa Starkey
Beth Helm
Teresa Reitnauer
C. Young
Amber Mancebo
Pros
Sharon Whatley, editing
Judy Bullard, cover design
Kyle Kane, logo design
Sabrina Wildermuth, design consultation

To those whose jobs entail seeking and upholding truth, justice, and honor.

*V*eronica Valencia walked into her hotel room, bed already turned down, fluffy white towels on a chair outside the bathroom, and inhaled deeply as she shut the door behind her. She loved the smell of a clean, well-scrubbed room. The reek of decay and despair on her last assignment had made her feel like crawling out of her own skin. She rolled her small suitcase into the bedroom closet and put her leather handbag on the glass coffee table in the room's sitting area. Then she walked to the floor-to-ceiling windows and looked out at the Los Angeles city lights.

She slipped out of her gray snakeskin heels and wiggled her toes. Then she splayed her hands on the window's glass and leaned forward, searching the skyline for the Hollywood sign. When she saw it, the vision always gave her a ripple of excitement.

A soft rap on the door pulled her back to the present. Dinner. She thought about grabbing her gun, but decided it wasn't necessary. Peering through the peephole, she saw a waiter with a cart. She pulled open the door.

"Ms. Ortiz? I've got your dinner here," said the young man, his smile eager and his eyes bright.

"Thank you, please come in," she said, stepping out of the way for him to enter. She checked behind him to make sure no one lurked in the hallway. As he pushed the cart in, she admired his good looks and wondered if it was true that everyone in LA was a hopeful actor.

"You can just leave the cart," she said, then reached for her purse and pulled out a tip.

His face lit up at the generous amount. "If there's anything else—"

"I'll let you know." She cut him off.

When he left, she pulled the lid off her plate to see salmon on a bed of rice and bright green broccoli. Finally, a decent meal. She could have been more adventuresome here in LA, but a nourishing meal was a huge step up from the swill she'd been eating.

She pulled a manila envelope out of her bag. Then she sat down at the table and poured herself a glass of chilled pinot grigio from the minibar. Taking a long, slow sip, she savored the dry flavor. Then she took a bite of salmon and opened the envelope. Pulling out two sheaths of paper, she shook them open, then laid them flat on the table next to her plate.

As she chewed, she studied the face of the man staring back at her. He had a strong jaw, and his green eyes danced, as if to say, *catch me if you can.* Robert Anton Harroway.

Placing a burgundy lacquered nail on the page, she scanned his vitals. Six foot three, two-hundred pounds. Harroway looked muscular, in good shape, dark hair, a little more ear than she personally liked, but ruggedly handsome. Known associates: some of the most powerful forces in British Intelligence. Graduated from Harvard with a degree in History. Veronica raised an eyebrow. Now that was interesting. She drained her glass of pinot. No recorded birthplace or family.

She picked up the other paper. This dossier was especially spotty. Clyde Amos Campo. Birth records said he was born in London, but no parents listed. Suspected as MI6 with British Intelligence, but nothing to confirm that. In addition to finding Harroway and compromising him for information, she'd been tasked with finding out more about Campo. Several raps on the door had Veronica folding the paperwork and sliding it back into the envelope and into her purse. Then she pulled out her beretta and held it close against her leg. She padded softly to the door, then looked through the spyhole.

Robert Harroway hung up from an exasperating call and sighed. Pushing his unruly black locks out of his eyes, he corralled his hair with a brown hair tie, then began tapping his foot. His superiors at MI6 wanted him to stay put. The argument was that if the CIA found him now, he'd be holed up in an interrogation room with their operatives for days, enduring who knew what kind of head games. The last time that had happened, he came away with a three-inch scar on his scalp.

He went to the window of the cottage and looked out at the meadow aglow in the morning light. Buttercups would soon fill the field with their spring cheer, and the days would warm. The director had told him to take it easy until they could further assess the CIA threat. That was a foreign concept to Robert. His personal cellphone pinged, and the display read: *Sassafras*.

He answered.

"Uncle?"

"What are you doing calling, little bug? Does your mummy know?"

"I don't know where she is."

Robert tensed. "How long has she been gone, Sassy?" He heard his niece crying on the other end of the line.

"Since after dinner. She said she'd be back in an hour."

Robert calculated the time in Los Angeles. Ten at night.

"Are you alone?"

"Yes, Mrs. Peters is off today."

"Have you tried calling Mummy, luv?"

"Over and over. But she doesn't answer."

Robert began gathering his things, throwing them into his bag. "I'm on my way. Do you remember about the safe room?"

"I think so."

"I need you to go in there right away. Do you understand? Go to the floorboard under your mother's bed and push on that button like we showed you." He waited. "Are you there yet?"

"I'm looking for Mr. Giraffe."

"I'll find him when I get there. It's important you get into the safe room right away."

"But—"

"Now, Sassy. No more tarrying," he said sharply, stopping to stand in the middle of the cottage, his bag tightly gripped in one hand, the phone in the other.

"I hear something. I think someone is at the door."

The muscles pulsated in Robert's neck. "Are you at the button?"

"Yes, I pushed it, but it won't open," the little girl said, anxiety in her voice.

"Push really hard."

"It opened."

"Get in now and push the lever inside. Quickly."

Robert waited, hoping, praying that she got in. He was silent, not wanting to distract her. Finally, when he thought he might burst, she said, "The door closed, Uncle Robert."

He let out a huge breath. "Do not leave that room. And stay very, very quiet. "

"I know," she said.

"It will take me lots of hours but I'll be there as fast as I can. You'll need to sleep in the safe room tonight. Okay?"

"Yes," came the small voice.

"I'll see you sometime late tomorrow. I'll open the door and come get you," he promised and hung up.

Then he rushed to Toulouse-Blagnac Airport. It would take him fourteen hours to get from France to Los Angeles. Robert prayed that his seven-year-old niece would stay in the safe room in the meantime.

*V*eronica relaxed her grip on the gun and opened the door.

"Horatio, this is a surprise." She stepped back.

Her handler strolled into the hotel room, trailing in the odor of cologne. He wore a black jacket and dark dress pants, a white shirt and red bow tie. His face was clean-shaven, except for a pencil-thin mustache.

"I was in the neighborhood at the opera. Rigoletto." Horatio lifted the wine bottle from the table and studied its label, then put it down. "I have some intel that just came in." He looked at Veronica. "Harroway may be coming to you."

Veronica set her gun down and reached for her glass of wine and refilled it. "That sounds promising."

"Word has it that one of his aliases was used to book a flight from the south of France to LAX. He arrives tomorrow afternoon at three."

Veronica took a sip of wine and replied, "Did we have something to do with his crawling out of the woodwork?"

Horatio stuck a hand in his jacket pocket and rattled keys. "No, the agency has no idea what or who smoked him out.

Harroway, as you know, is slippery. With whatever wildcard this is thrown in the mix, you won't know what to expect."

Veronica thought about taking another sip of wine, but stopped herself. She elongated her body, her eyes meeting Horatio's. "Thank you for your concern, but I'll be fine."

"I hope so," said Horatio, his height bearing down on her. She wished she hadn't taken off her heels now. "The last operation—I had to clean up the mess you left." His gray eyes warned her. "I don't like messes. Especially when they end with me benched. And you coming out without a scratch. We know why."

A flash of irritation coursed through Veronica, and with deliberate intent she drew nearer to Horatio. "If you're referring to my father and his influence, I don't mix family with work. Has it occurred to you that you were benched because you deserved it?"

Veronica stood unmoving, daring Horatio to say more. When he didn't, she smiled. "Just think, you wouldn't have time for the opera if you were still in the field."

Anger crossed Horatio's face, then he stepped back and looked down at his watch. "I must go. Let me know the moment you make contact with Harroway."

Horatio left, closing the door behind him. Veronica deadbolted and latched it.

Robert stowed his bag in the overhead bin and sat down next to the window. He looked outside as the plane's engine whined and reassured himself. Sassy was a smart girl. She would stay put for now. But where the hell was Fiona? He felt certain his sister would never leave Sassy alone. Unless something was terribly wrong. Anxiety twisted a knot in his stomach, and he tapped his foot, anxious for the plane to be in the air.

When they took off a few minutes later, Robert tried to sit back and relax, but he couldn't help worrying that Fiona's ex had found her. Robert and his Uncle Campo had been careful to help her start a new life in the States, but Sassy's father was as resourceful as he was dangerous. And by now he would be furious with Fiona for fleeing.

Horatio's presence still lingered in Veronica's hotel room. As she finished her meal, she became increasingly more irritated with her handler. She was tired of hearing about the last mission. Horatio wasn't the one who had to put up with the disgusting cult leader's manhandling. Revulsion coursed through her every time she thought of the man's hot, clammy hands on her. True, she'd dealt with this sort of thing all her life, but she never got used to it.

"Come, V, your father and I need you at the dinner table."
"I told Madeline to tell you I'm not feeling well."

Sixteen at the time, Veronica had burrowed herself under her covers. She pulled her duvet up under her chin.

Dressed in a black, flowing gown, her platinum blond hair twisted into a bun on the top of her head, her mother came to put a cool, slim hand on Veronica's brow. "You don't feel hot."

"It's that filthy Spanish ambassador. You know he keeps looking at me. That's the only reason he comes here every chance he gets."

"Veronica, your father has work to do with him. But, yes, I see how he looks at you. Just ignore him."

"It's hard to ignore his leering face. He makes me feel like throwing up."

Her mother sighed. "This agreement with the Spanish government is important. Please do this for your father and I, one more time. I'll take you to Paris for a shopping spree. Just you and me."

Veronica felt the familiar tug of giving into her mother. "Can we go to Angelina's for hot chocolate?"

"Of course," her mother said. "Now get up and come to dinner."

Veronica sighed and pulled back the covers, getting out of bed.

"That's not the formal dress I got you for tonight," her mother said of the bright pink turtleneck and black slacks Veronica wore.

"The less the ambassador sees of me, the better. And if you leave me in the room with him alone, don't blame me if he ends up with a salad fork in his pudgy hand."

Her mother ran her fingers through Veronica's brown, curly hair, then pushed her bangs out of her eyes. "The things you say, V. Some mothers would be concerned."

Veronica ate the roll that had come with the salmon as she looked over the dossiers again. She memorized what little information they had, then went into the bathroom and opened the toilet bowl. Tearing the papers into tiny pieces, she threw them in and flushed.

3

*W*hen the plane touched down in Los Angeles, Robert waited for the all-clear, hopeful everyone would stay seated long enough for him to make it at least partway down the aisle. Unless there was a traffic gridlock, he'd be at Fiona's house in Santa Monica in less than thirty minutes. He grabbed his bag and squeezed his way past annoyed passengers pulling their luggage out of overhead bins. Once in the terminal, he took long strides toward the exit.

Where was he going in such a hurry? Veronica practically ran to keep up with Harroway as he walked through the automatic glass doors. Tall and well-built, with long, determined steps, he kept up his brisk pace down the sidewalk.

She raced to the car she had hired waiting at the curb and slipped into the back seat.

"Where to?" The driver looked at her in the rearview mirror. The cab smelled of garlic.

"Where's the long-term parking?"

"Up a level."

"Go there."

Harroway had disappeared from view. Veronica hoped she was right about him having a car parked. Trying to find him in this city of four million people was going to be impossible if she lost him now.

Robert paid the attendant a handsome tip, hoping that would put him first in line to get his car. While he waited, he tried calling Sassy. The phone went straight to voicemail. He knew better than to leave a message. Within a couple of minutes, his Mercedes approached. The attendant got out of the car and handed him the key with a smile.

Hopping in, he threw his bag on the passenger seat, then headed out of the parking lot. A couple of turns and he was driving up Pacific Coast Highway. The day was bright and clear and the traffic was moving. He reached into the glovebox and took out his sunglasses.

When his cellphone buzzed, he yanked it out of his pocket. A text read: *Word has it you've made a move. What happened to staying put?* Robert threw the phone on the seat. He checked his mirror. A sedan had been following him since he left the parking lot. If he had more time, he'd pull off the road to lose the car, but today he didn't even have seconds to spare.

Veronica wished she were driving. Harroway had to have spotted them by now. At this rate, she'd be having her confrontation with the man sooner than later. Veronica didn't like that. She preferred to stalk her prey for a while. Get to know their habits and proclivities. It made it easier to compromise them. She sat back in her seat and smoothed her skirt. Then she took out her compact and applied more burgundy lipstick, all the while keeping her eyes on Harroway's car.

When they arrived in Santa Monica, he pulled off onto a side street. "Keep following the Mercedes," she ordered. "Try to hang back some."

The driver slowed the car as they continued to follow. When they came to a quiet, tree-lined neighborhood, she said, "Stop the car." The driver hit the brakes. Veronica watched as Harroway's car continued, then drove into the driveway of a house. Was he meeting a lover, perhaps? Or a fellow spy?

Robert parked in Fiona's driveway and checked out the

sedan now stopped some distance away. He'd have to deal with whomever that was once he had Sassy safely in tow. He went around to the trunk and opened it, then reached into where the spare tire was kept for his handgun. Then he headed for the front door, which he found ajar. His heart began to pound, and he prayed his niece had not been detected. With his foot, he pushed the door open quietly, then entered, gun drawn. He locked the door behind him to keep out whoever was in the car. In the living room, he found his sister's rolltop desk opened and some paperwork strewn on the floor. As he checked the house, Robert stopped every now and then and listened for any movement. In the kitchen, last night's dinner dishes sat on the table. Sassy's favorite cup still contained some milk.

He checked the laundry room off the kitchen and the den. Then he scanned the small yard and pool. Nothing.

At the winding staircase, he made his way up the stairs, holding his breath, straining to detect any sounds. Still nothing. The first room to the right, the guest bedroom, was empty. Same with the bathroom off the hallway, and Fiona's office. Then he came to Sassy's room. All quiet in there, except for stuffed animals and several dolls scattered on the floor. He opened the closet and checked under the bed, then the linen closet in the hallway. The last room, his sister's, sent his blood racing. He entered, afraid of what he might see, but nothing appeared to be touched. Assured now that no one was in the house, he reached under the bed and pushed the button on the floorboard. The door to the safe room slid open.

"The meter's ticking, lady. You're up to thirty bucks."

"You'll be paid."

The driver turned on his radio.

"Turn that off."

When he huffed, she added, "I'll pay you extra for the silence."

Her phone buzzed, and she pulled it out of her bag. A text from Horatio. *Contact made?* She returned her cell to her purse. "I'll be back in a while," she told the driver. "When I return, be ready to head out quickly."

"Look, I'm not going to be the getaway car if you're planning on robbing someone."

Veronica reached into her wallet and pulled out a hundred-dollar bill. She slapped it into his hand. "I've got plenty of money. I'm not robbing anyone. Just be ready."

She got out and began walking toward the house, one hand in her purse holding her gun. Knowing Harroway's reputation, she could be walking straight into an ambush.

4

*R*obert kneeled in front of his niece, who he'd found crouched in the corner of the safe room. Taking her in his arms, he soothed, "It's okay."

After a time, her heart stopped pitter-pattering madly against his chest and her trembling subsided. He loosened his grip and looked at her face, covered in red blotches and wet with tears. "Uncle Robert's here now," he said, then pushed a lock of blond hair out of her eyes.

"Did you find Mommy?" she asked hopefully.

"Not yet, little bug, but I will." He looked around the room, spying a soda on the table. "Have you had anything to eat or drink since we talked last night?"

She shook her head. "Only a little soda. There were some cans in the cabinet. I'm not too hungry."

"We're going on an adventure. How about we get you a snack and a water from the cupboard, and we'll take it with us. I think eating something will make you feel better."

"Are we going to find Mommy?"

"First, we're going to get you somewhere safe. Then I'll find your mother."

Robert waited while the little girl thought about what he said. "Can I get Mr. Giraffe from my room?"

"Of course. I'll go with you to find him, and we'll grab some clothing. You can change out of your pjs."

His niece started for the door, but he stopped her. "Let me go first."

When her eyes widened and tears threatened, he assured her. "Everything is going to be fine." He stepped out into the bedroom and listened. No sounds, but he was still thinking of the sedan that had been following him. He went to the window and looked down the street. The car was gone.

"Is it okay to come out?" Sassy's tiny voice asked from the safe room.

"Yes, luv, but let's hurry, shall we?"

Sassy ran out with a water bottle and bag of nuts clutched in one hand, while Robert opened the panel and entered the password to close the safe room. Then he led her to her bedroom where he pulled down a bag from the top shelf of the closet. "Throw in some undies, pants, tops, sweaters, like what you wear to school," he instructed. "And don't forget an extra pair of shoes and a fresh pair of pjs."

Sassy pulled on pants and a t-shirt with colorful purple and pink butterflies on the front, then removed clothing from her dresser and grabbed a bedraggled, stuffed giraffe from the floor by the bed. Robert took the clothing and placed it in the bag, then gently put the giraffe on top and zipped. "Grab your toothbrush on the way out," he said.

When they got to the stairway, Robert halted Sassy and listened again. Then he took her hand and said, "We're going to run to the car, okay? See who is fastest."

Sassy gave him a worried look.

"Uncle Robert needs some exercise."

Sassy grinned. "I'm going to beat you!" Then she flew down the stairs with Robert following her.

When they got to the car, he checked the back seat, then motioned for her to get in the front next to him. Quickly backing out of the driveway, he looked around for the suspicious sedan. Whoever was tailing him appeared to be gone.

When Veronica first arrived at the house, she slipped along the side, walking quietly, listening. She then peered in the downstairs windows. No one in the living room or dining room. Around the west side of the house, she came to a set of closed blinds. She took a listening device out of her purse and put the earbuds in, then placed the unit against the glass, and turned it on. Nothing distinguishable. She spied a ladder in the neighbor's yard sitting against a shed and looked up at the second story. Then she had another thought. Maybe in his haste, her mark had left something in the car.

She went back to the front of the house and found the car unlocked. Glancing up at the curtained windows, she didn't see anyone. She opened the door as quietly as possible, then checked under the seats and in the glove compartment. Nothing of importance. Then she pulled the trunk lever. When she went around the back of the car, she glanced down the street and gasped. Her driver had left! She should never have given him money. She lifted the trunk lid to take a look and jumped when she heard the door to the house open and a young girl's voice. With a fraction of a second to make a decision, she hopped in the trunk and pulled the lid shut with a click.

"I think someone is calling you, Uncle Robert," said Sassy as they drove north on Pacific Coast Highway.

Robert pulled his cellphone out of his pocket. Headquarters again. He pressed answer.

"Tell me you have a perfectly good reason for disobeying a direct order."

"I do," Robert said.

"Care to elaborate?"

Robert glanced at Sassy munching on nuts.

"I need some personal time."

"You're the subject of a manhunt."

"I'll explain everything, but not now."

The director was silent. "How long to deal with your situation?"

"Two, three days."

"Make sure to check in regularly."

Robert agreed and hung up, then dialed another number. He needed answers.

Veronica shifted in the trunk, cramped and uncomfortable. Something hard was wedged into her back, and it smelled like oil in here. Her phone buzzed, and she frantically fished it out of her purse, turning it on mute. Another text from Horatio. He sent a question mark. She was about to answer, when the car went over railroad tracks, and the metal object dug into her back several times. She winced, then finished her text. *I've made contact.* Then she pushed send. After sliding her phone back into her purse, she took out her beretta, cold, silent, and reassuring, and cradled it in her hand. She'd be ready when Harroway opened the trunk.

"V, your principal called me. You were in another argument with the Holmes boy?"

Veronica had been summoned to the living room expecting to see her father, but her mother was there alone, sitting on the brocade sofa.

"Where's Father?"

"He had a last minute flight to catch."

Veronica tried to hide her disappointment, but blurted, "I barely saw him, and now he's gone again."

"Back to your argument with that boy."

"Bobby is a bully. He's constantly bugging me and some of the other girls. I put him in his place. Next time he'll keep his fat mouth shut."

Her mother reached for her cup of tea and took a sip. When she set it back down, the cup rattled on the saucer. She finally spoke. "This has been happening far too often. You're in sixth grade now. It's time to start acting like it. I'm going to have to tell your father about this."

Good, thought Veronica. Then she'd finally have his attention.

5

"*W*here are we going, Uncle Robert?"

"I'm taking you to a friend's house in the mountains."

"The lady with the puppy?"

"You remember her? That was a long time ago."

Sassy clapped her hands. "Does she still have the puppy?"

Robert laughed. "The puppy is a big dog now, I imagine."

Sassy turned toward her uncle, eyes serious. "Then you'll go find Mommy?"

"Yes, Sassafras."

The car started to climb as they headed into the Santa Monica Mountains. Hillsides dotted with coastal sagebrush were soon replaced with the intense yellows of wild mustard. After a time, the terrain became dense with towering trees. Robert turned off the road onto a rocky dirt path that had the car bumping up and down past the twisted beauty of native wild oaks until they came to a cabin. He let the car roll to a stop as he looked at the old place, thinking back to nights spent talking on the porch. He had always loved the way moonlight filtered through the trees here, and let the memories of another time fill him.

Just as he shut off the engine, the front door opened, and a woman walked out onto the porch. Her broad smile lit up her eyes. She crossed fleshy arms over a bright green apron and rocked back on her heels, delight on her face. Robert could smell something delicious wafting from the cabin as he and Sassy got out of the car and walked toward her. For a moment he felt shocked to see the woman's hair now gone totally gray, then it seemed as if it had always been that way.

"I was surprised to get your call," she said, meeting Robert's eyes as he climbed the steps, then added quickly, "But I'm not complaining."

"It's been too long, Helga."

"No matter, I know your work keeps you busy." Then she drew her attention to Sassy. "My, have you grown, child!"

The little girl looked up at Helga and gave her a shy smile.

"She remembers your dog. Do you still have him?"

"Lumpy? Why sure, I do. He's inside doing what he does best—snoozing." She took Sassy's hand. "Come on in, and we'll wake him up. I'm cooking some stew for dinner. Do you like stew? I know your Uncle Robert does."

When the car came to a stop and two doors opened and slammed shut, Veronica tried to hear what was being said outside, but couldn't make anything out. Wherever they now were, they seemed to have traveled over an unpaved road to get here. Had he stopped for the night? One thing Veronica knew for sure. She wasn't going to spend the night in the trunk. She rummaged around in her bag and pulled out her lockpick, then turned on her cellphone flashlight and began picking the trunk lock—a skill she was grateful, at the moment, to have acquired.

After they finished eating, Robert started to remove his bowl, but Helga stopped him. "Go on now. I know you have pressing matters. I just wanted to get your belly full before you set out."

Robert pushed himself back from the table. "I haven't had something that good in a long time, Helga. Thank you. I'll be back as soon as possible."

"With Mommy, right?" said Sassy.

"That's right." He leaned over and kissed the top of her head.

"How's about a piece of blueberry pie, Sassy?" said Helga as Robert stood up to leave.

The little girl nodded vigorously. "With ice cream?"

Helga got up from her chair. "Of course." She turned to face Robert, who came around the table and gave her a quick hug.

"Thank you," he said.

Helga searched his eyes. "Have you—?"

"Seen him? Not recently, but I did track him to South America not long ago. Last I heard, he was okay. I left a message for him on the way here."

Relief covered her face. "And now you have a new missing person to find," she said in a low voice.

"I'll find her."

Helga gave him a small smile and put out her hand to cradle one of his cheeks. "Such a hard and busy life you lead, Robbie. Will you ever settle down, do you think?"

He smiled and chuckled. "Not likely."

The woman grinned. "Now there's that daredevil smile. Take that with you, and Godspeed."

Veronica just about had the trunk lock picked when a car door opened and the engine started up. "Dammit," she muttered, bracing herself for another painful ride.

The car drove for what seemed like an eternity, and Veronica found herself yawning. What was wrong with her? She could stay awake in the past for two days straight waiting to compromise a target.

"You're home from your trip. You can come to my ballet recital tonight."

It was a Friday morning, and Veronica was on her way to school. They were living in Italy at the time. Her father sat in his study; his glasses perched on the end of his nose as he read the newspaper. He looked up at Veronica and frowned. "You're dancing? What happened to playing the piano?"

"I took piano in London. I'm 'expanding my horizons,' like you suggested."

He cocked his head to one side as he often did. "There's something to be said for consistency, Veronica. I have an engagement tonight, so I won't be able to see your performance. I'm sure you'll do well." Then he turned the page of the newspaper and went back to reading.

Veronica gulped back the tears that threatened to spill and left the house. She'd have to ask Mother about taking piano again.

Robert noticed that the car seemed to be making a tapping noise he hadn't heard before. He'd have to take it into the shop. Just then his phone buzzed. He grabbed it. "Uncle Campo, you got my message," he said.

"I did. No word about Fiona?"

"None. Where are you?"

"I should be there by tomorrow. Your ETA?"

"About twenty minutes from the safe house," said Robert.

"And Sassy?"

"She's secure with Helga."

Silence on the other end of the line. "How is Helga?"

"A rock, as always."

"I'm checking with all of my sources regarding your sister. I'm sure you've done the same."

Worry tightened in Robert's chest. "Yes, of course."

"We'll find her."

Robert hoped his Uncle Campo was right. He shut off the

phone and focused on the sign he was about to pass. Twenty miles to Oxnard. Once at the safe house, he could do a more thorough check with his sources using the secure satellite.

When he pulled into a residential neighborhood five blocks from the ocean, Robert slowed the car, soon approaching a narrow, two-story house. He got out and pressed a code onto a keypad, which opened the garage door. Then he pulled into the tight space and turned off the car. Carefully opening the driver's side door, he squeezed out. After pressing a button to shut the garage door, he hedged his way to the back and crouched down to peer beneath the car, looking for anything obvious that might be causing the tapping sound. He noticed what could be dripping. Best to pull out the tarp he kept in the trunk to protect the floor.

6

*R*obert opened the car trunk and jumped. He looked closer, sure he'd seen just about everything in his line of work, but this was a first. Lying in the trunk of his car, body curved in a fetal position, was an unconscious woman. She held a beretta in her hands. He looked around as if expecting someone to suddenly appear from the shadows and solve this riddle. What the fuck was going on?

Robert pressed two fingers over her wrist pulse. She was alive. He slipped the gun out of her grasp and set it to the side. Then he called for her to open her eyes and tried to shake her awake. No response. There were no signs of blood. Then he realized with a shock that the pinging could be a sign of an exhaust leak. The carbon monoxide may have made its way to the trunk. He pulled his phone out and dialed in a number.

"Hans," the man answered.

"It's Robert. I'm relieved you picked up."

"It's been a long time, friend."

"Are you at the medical center right now?"

"Yes. What's wrong?"

"I think it's carbon monoxide poisoning."

"Who?"

"A woman. Thirty-something years old. She's unresponsive."

"You still on 22nd near the beach?"

"Yes."

"I'll be there in ten. Get her into fresh air—now!"

Robert put his phone away, then picked the woman up. He carried her into the house, kicking the door to the garage closed behind them. Then he laid her on the sofa, slipped a pillow beneath her head, and opened the patio door and several windows to allow a flow of fresh air. The woman's skin was flushed. He checked her pulse again and was relieved to still feel one. Unsure of what to do next, he started pacing in front of her. Who on earth was she? Why and how did she crawl into his trunk? He'd seen a purse next to her in the car but would wait until Hans was here with her to retrieve it and get some information on her.

True to his word, Hans was soon at the front door. He wore blue scrubs and had an oxygen machine that Robert helped him wheel in. "Attach the mask to the tubing there and plug the machine into the wall," he ordered Robert. "I need to check her vitals." Hans kneeled beside the woman and lifted first one lid, then the other, to check her eyes. He put his ear to her chest. While Robert was readying the machine, Hans took her blood pressure. "Where did she get the carbon monoxide poisoning?"

"In the trunk of my car."

Hans narrowed his eyes and looked at Robert as if he were speaking some other language. "Well, that sucks. Do tell."

Robert held up his hands. "I had no idea she was in there."

"You still have that ancient Mercedes?" Hans shook his

head. "Never mind, I know you do." He wheeled the oxygen machine next to the woman, then fitted the mask over her face. The machine buzzed when he turned it on and began pumping air.

"Is she going to be okay?" said Robert, taking a good look at her for the first time. She had a mass of brown, shoulder-length hair, and flawless porcelain skin. She looked well-dressed and wore a burgundy-colored skirt and gray silk blouse tied in a soft bow at her neck. One of her heels must have fallen off when he brought her into the house. Her slender foot was bare, her toenails painted red.

"A hyperbaric oxygen treatment would be best, but I feel confident she'll be okay with this," said Hans, checking the valves. "I know you can't reveal much, but what's your guess as to how long she was in your trunk?"

Robert shrugged his shoulders, then frowned and chewed at his bottom lip.

Hans chuckled. "Always a dramatic entrance with you, Harroway." He checked her pulse again and nodded in approval. "Stronger, that's good." He remained squatting beside the woman, his forearms resting on his thighs.

"I was grateful to catch you," said Robert. "Otherwise, it would have been the paramedics and police with questions I don't have answers to. Some part of this wasn't by accident. I just don't know if she crawled in, or someone put her there."

"Good thing I was still at the hospital. I told them that my old maid aunt needed some emergency oxygen." He smiled. "But anything happens to the machinery; you owe me five grand."

"Well, let's make sure nothing does. How long does she need to be on that thing?" asked Robert.

"At least four or five hours, so it's going to be a long night."

Robert went to the garage and recovered the woman's

purse and stray shoe from the trunk. He picked up the pistol and set the safety, then slid it into the back of his pants. Once inside, he went into a back bedroom and flipped on the light. Then he emptied the contents of her purse onto the bed. Lipstick and a compact. A wallet containing a fair amount of cash. He also found a US passport with her photo and the name Sylvia Ortiz. The passport had a holographic overlay, so it was either real or a government agency issued passport with a fake name. Her cellphone was not surprisingly locked. He tried various configurations, but nothing would unlock it. There were two items of particular interest—what appeared to be a listening device and a lock pick. He'd have to wait until his mystery guest woke up to find out who she was and what she wanted.

It was midnight when the woman began murmuring in her sleep. Robert sat up from the armchair where he'd been dozing and Hans rose from the recliner and went to check her vitals again, nodding in approval as he did so. "We don't want to be premature, but this is promising," Hans said, then went to lie back down. "Remember when we stayed up for days studying for finals?" he said as he made himself comfortable.

Robert laughed. "You mean you stayed up for days studying."

"I think I'm still making up for all that lost sleep. That and my time as a resident." Hans shut his eyes. "Wake me up if she does."

As his friend quickly went back to sleep, Robert thought of their time together as Harvard schoolmates. They'd met at the library one day during their freshman year, and immediately hit it off. In their sophomore year, they began rooming together. The years they spent together in school sealed their friendship. Hans was a much more dedicated student than Robert, always hitting the books and fiercely dedicated to his studies. Everyone would take off to drink beer until two in the morning, but Hans always stayed behind in their room and would still be working when Robert returned. He felt glad for that now.

The woman whimpered. Robert watched closely as she slept, her rhythmic, somewhat slow breathing becoming irregular, her eyes moving rapidly beneath closed lids. He leaned closer, concerned, but soon she quieted down. Relaxing back in the chair, he planned on a light sleep for himself. Robert would be right here the minute she woke up. He had a lot of questions for Sleeping Beauty.

Veronica's eyes felt heavy. She tried to open them, aware of a strange whirring sound nearby, but found herself drifting again. Her father was with her, sitting in the front row as part of an audience in a palace, witnessing a coronation. A man in a flowing, white robe held a crown, and the woman seated had bowed her head, waiting for him to place the crown. Veronica felt so happy to be with her father, since it was rare for him to take time out of his busy schedule to be with her. She proudly admired her black patent shoes and favorite blue dress. Her father turned his head and met her eyes, nodding in approval. Veronica smiled up at him, an elated feeling that she mattered bubbling in her chest. But then her father pointed to her shoes, and her stomach clenched. They didn't match. One shoe was perfect, shiny, and black, but the other shoe was brown and badly scuffed.

Through tears she suddenly noticed her beautiful dress was torn. She tried to tuck the material beneath one leg to hide it, but her father saw, his brows crossing into a frown as he shook his head in disapproval.

"I'll fix it, Father," she cried as the tears kept growing. "Just give me a minute. Please." But when she looked up, he was gone, and she sat alone in the crowd.

WHEN VERONICA OPENED HER EYES, she blinked at the strong stream of light filling the room. A strange sound of mechanical pumping filled her ears. What was on her face? She grasped the mask and pulled it off. Where the hell was she? She started to sit up, but dizziness overcame her, and she flopped back down.

"Good morning," said a voice.

Veronica looked up into green eyes and gasped.

7

The man Veronica knew to be Harroway said in an English accent, "Who are you? And what were you doing in my trunk?"

Veronica struggled to sit up. "Where's my gun?"

Harroway reached out and touched her arm. "Your gun is safe, but you almost died with it."

Veronica rested back on the couch. She tried to piece together what had happened. She remembered getting into his trunk, but it became blurry after that. Harroway continued to study her, and she felt his intense scrutiny to be unnerving.

"I'm not going to get up," she snapped. "Can you please give me some breathing room."

Harroway stepped back a few paces as another man walked into the room. He had close-cropped blond hair and wore scrubs and moved with assurance. "You're awake," he said in an American accent. He pulled out a stethoscope, which he started to put to her chest.

"What are you doing?" Veronica pulled away.

The man glanced at Harroway, then back at Veronica.

"Carbon monoxide poisoning is serious business. I'm just going to check your vitals."

"What?" she said, incredulous.

"Why don't you get us some coffee while I check her?" the doctor suggested to Harroway.

When he left, Veronica asked, "How long was I unconscious?"

The man put the stethoscope to her chest and listened. Then he took her wrist in his hand and checked the watch on his arm. He nodded, satisfied, then replied, "About eight hours."

"Will there be any long-term effects?" she asked.

He shook his head. "I don't think so. You are lucky, though. If Robert hadn't found you when he did, you wouldn't have made it. I'd advise resting a few more hours before resuming normal activities."

"How much do I owe you?"

The man unplugged the machine she'd been hooked up to and gathered his things. "Robert took care of it." He wagged a finger at her. "No more riding around in car trunks." Then he turned and wheeled the machine out of the room. "Especially of old Mercedes," he called over his shoulder.

After he'd left, Veronica sat up and tried to stand, but the room tilted, so she sat back down.

Harroway entered with two cups of coffee. He set one on the table, then sat down across from her in an armchair.

What a mess this was, Veronica thought. She'd lost all hope of taking him off guard. And now he had her gun. "Where are my things?" she demanded. "I need to be on my way."

"Just like that?" Harroway smiled. "Without an explanation as to how you ended up in my trunk?"

"It was an accident."

Harroway nodded toward the coffee on the table. "It's

black. Somehow you don't seem like the cream and sugar type."

He was right. Veronica reached over and took the cup in her hands, which shook slightly. She sipped the dark, aromatic liquid. When the warmth settled in her stomach, she said, "My name is Sylvia Ortiz. I have money in my bag. I'll pay you for the doctor's services. Then as soon as I feel steady, I'll leave."

Harroway leaned forward and set his coffee cup on the table between them. He wore dark slacks and a pale-yellow Oxford shirt unbuttoned at the neck. His sleek, black hair was pulled back into a ponytail. "If your job were to kill me, you would have tried already," he said. "So that tells me you're looking for information."

Veronica knew she'd been caught and nothing she could say would seem plausible. She had put herself in such a compromising position. But she couldn't go back to Horatio empty-handed.

As if reading her mind, Harroway said, "Your situation is not something you'd want to tell your superiors, I imagine. You're obviously CIA. I assume you want to know what the MI6 has uncovered about threats against the life of your country's secretary of defense. Yet I've got more pressing matters to attend to."

Veronica tried to hide her surprise. If the US Secretary of Defense was in danger, then her father would know about it, as well. But Horatio didn't bother to tell her.

Robert watched the woman, whose eyes were unusually

expressive. He could tell when he mentioned the secretary of defense that she had heard nothing about it prior. He leaned back in his seat. "I used to do that," he said.

"Do what?"

"Take orders blindly. Go ahead. Call your boss and ask about the threat."

"You seem to be in possession of my phone," she said, managing to sit up and set the coffee cup down.

"You appear to be starting to feel like yourself," he said. "Though you certainly had no business being in my trunk, I do apologize that my car nearly killed you."

She ran her hands down her hair but didn't respond.

Every moment he sat here playing repartee with this woman, Robert thought, was a moment he could be looking for his sister. And if Sylvia, or whatever her name was, made a phone call to her superiors, this safe house would be exposed. Robert would have to stop her from making any calls or leaving.

8

*T*here was no way Harroway was going to let Veronica go just like that.

"Where is your restroom?" she asked.

He got up from the armchair. "I'll take you to it."

Veronica looked at her feet. "My shoes?"

Robert reached around the back of the couch and picked up her heels, handing them to her. Then he watched as she put them on and stood.

"No need. Just tell me where it is."

"You're recuperating," he said, his eyes daring her. He pointed to the hallway. "After you."

Veronica walked past him and headed down the hall. When they got to a door on the left, he reached around her and pulled it open. "I'll be right here."

After shutting the bathroom door behind her, Veronica stood still for a moment and listened. Silence. She turned on the faucet at the sink and glanced around the small space. There was a window, but even if she climbed through and ran, she couldn't leave without her purse. She opened the medicine chest, looking for something useful to use for an escape. Nothing but a bottle of aspirin and some Band-Aids.

Robert waited outside the bathroom. His uncle should be here soon. Maybe between the two of them they could figure out what to do with this woman. When she pulled the door open a few minutes later, Robert stepped back to let her pass. He noted her perfume, the scent of a single flower, maybe lilac or violet, and felt a desire to step closer to smell it again.

"Thank you so much for all of your trouble." Her words sounded forced, though she smiled politely. He had to admit, she did have a way about her, like a puma stalking its prey.

"Are you feeling up to leaving?" he asked.

She was about to answer when a car stopped outside. It didn't sound like his uncle's vehicle. Robert pulled her into the living room.

"What is it?" she said.

He opened the slats of the blind with two fingers and peered outside. A black sedan. "We have to get out of here. Come with me."

"I need my purse," she said.

"It's in the master bedroom. We're leaving from there."

In the bedroom, he directed them into the closet where he pulled up the carpeting and yanked open a trap door. With his cellphone, he lit up a passageway a few feet down just as the front door banged open. Footsteps entered the house. "Go!" said Robert. She lowered herself into the dank, dark passageway, and he climbed down behind her and shut the trapdoor. He shined his light down the tunnel and said, "Crawl forward."

They made their way through the narrow passage, barely big enough to fit them, even on all fours. When they got to another trapdoor, he reached above her and pushed it up. Sunlight shone in.

Veronica stood and quickly brushed the dirt from her skirt and hands, then pulled herself up through the passageway, and Robert followed. They emerged in an atrium filled with spidery ferns, philodendrons, and pots of exotic flowering plants.

"We're a few houses down now," Robert said. "Give me your purse."

She pulled it close to her chest. "You already have my gun."

"There's a tracker on you."

Veronica watched Harroway meticulously check inside her purse. Then he took out a pocketknife and slit the lining. She sucked in a breath when he extracted a small electronic device and held it up for her to see. He put a finger against his lips to warn her not to speak.

"I had no idea," she mouthed the words.

He smashed the device on the ground with his shoe, then picked up the remnants. "You figure out how it got there, and we'll know who our visitor is." He sat down on a wrought iron chair next to a small bistro table and took out his phone. After scrolling through some images, he held the phone up for her to see. "Do you recognize this man?"

Tall and bulky, with a large nose and pockmarked skin, the man stood in front of the couch she was just recovering on. He held a pistol with a silencer attached. Veronica felt her heart speed up at having come close to being on the receiving end of that pistol. "I don't know him."

Harroway's eyes darkened. "You have no idea who he is?"

She shrugged. "Should I?"

He muttered, entering more information into his phone. After a few moments, he raised his eyebrows.

"Well?" she said. "Who is he?"

He shot her a stormy look. "How about you tell me your real name, and I'll tell you who is trying to assassinate you?"

"Assassinate me? He broke into your house."

"That house was secure, until you came along. You're the one with the tracker."

"I told you, I'm Sylvia Orte—."

Robert stood up and faced her. His body tightened. "Rubbish," he said, moving closer as she backed into a potted plant. She glanced about her for a way out.

"Where are you going to run?" he asked.

He was so close now; she felt the heat from his body. Veronica had obviously been breached, and someone might want her dead. Harroway could have the answer in his hands. "Okay. My name is Veronica Valencia, and I am CIA."

Harroway studied her face. Her answer seemed to convince him because his shoulders slackened, and he backed up. "Your visitor is a known American assassin by the name of McElroy. Any idea why he's after you?"

For the first time since he'd met Veronica, Robert saw a chink in her armor. "Let's start again," he suggested. "Does the man look familiar?"

Veronica sighed. "Vaguely."

"Any idea who tracked your purse?"

"It's usually in my possession."

"The operative term being usually."

Robert waited for her to answer and was surprised when she suddenly blurted out, "The last person I saw was my handler."

"Do you have reason to distrust him?"

She looked uncomfortable. "He got benched because of something that happened during our last assignment, so he's my handler now. He's been angry about it."

Robert sat back down. "It seems he may be acting on that anger."

A frisson of fear swept through Veronica when she thought about how lethal Horatio could be.

9

*R*obert typed a text message to his uncle: *Location breached. At alternate location with an unexpected guest. Your ETA?*

Then he brought his attention back to Veronica. She sat erect on the chair next to him, not moving. Her eyes stared unblinking, somewhere in the distance, as if she were trying to work things out in her mind. The way she sat with her legs crossed at the ankle, hands folded in her lap, reminded Robert just how lovely she was. When she turned toward him, worry was etched across her face.

"I'm at a standstill," she said. "I have no idea who to call now that I suspect my handler of wanting me killed. When you lose confidence in those around you, there's not much left." A sense of apprehension colored her words. She put the palms of her hands together, then pressed the sides of her index fingers against her lips. Finally, she dropped her hands back into her lap. She turned and studied him for a moment. "If you know that the CIA is after you to gain information about the threat on our secretary of defense, why are you in the US?"

"I have something to take care of here," he said, checking his phone again. Time was not on his side. Go ahead and leave, he thought. I'm not going to stop you.

"Who are we waiting for?" she asked.

"Another operative. He should have been here by now." Veronica was becoming inquisitive, he thought. Something he didn't have time to deal with.

"It seems we're at an impasse," said Veronica. She leaned back in her chair.

Robert put down his phone and mimicked her actions. "It seems that we are. I'm certain you have your order to acquire what information you can from me. And I can only wonder at what else you have on your agenda."

"It seems you're pretty concerned about someone or something," said Veronica.

Robert sighed, worry gnawing at his stomach.

"Perhaps I can help? We are in my territory, after all," said Veronica. "A quid pro quo."

Harroway looked like he was about to answer Veronica when there was a sound outside the atrium. He pulled his gun and pointed it at the door, which slowly opened. When he saw who it was, he put the gun down. "Finally, I was beginning to wonder," he said to the man. Veronica couldn't help but feel delighted at her luck. Her other target, Clyde Campo, stood there. The older man had a shock of short-cropped hair and wore trousers and a black turtleneck, laced boots on his feet. A pair of glasses hung around his neck.

Campo's eyes darted from Harroway to Veronica, and

then he exclaimed, "What the bloody hell are you doing with her?"

Harroway sat up in his chair.

"She's the daughter of the director of the Defense Intelligence Agency," Campo continued. "Not to mention, she's CIA."

Harroway looked genuinely surprised. His eyes swept her face before directing his gaze back at Campo. "I knew she was with the agency, but I didn't know her father headed the DIA. That explains why she's so interested in who is after her country's secretary of defense. Although, you'd think the CIA would have its own intel."

Veronica felt stupid. "Of course, we have good intel," she said. "But we obviously need to know more, which is where you come in."

Campo held up his cellphone. "We must get out of here immediately. I have the chap in the safe house on my webcam, and he's still prowling about."

Harroway stood. "Alright then." He looked at Veronica. "Are you coming, or will you wait for the mercenary?"

Veronica thought about her choice. She would like to confront the hired gun and find out who sent him after her, but if she let Harroway and Campo go, she would lose them.

"I'll come with you," she said, standing.

Harroway gestured for her to follow Campo. As he did so, a surge of intrigue coursed through Veronica. And she was rarely ever intrigued.

"V, how could you? He's the French ambassador's son," said Veronica's mother.

Veronica sat at her dressing table in her room at the Buenos Aires embassy. She looked at her mother's reflection in the mirror. They'd only been there a month, but her mother had already seen to it that she'd made her rounds with the embassy's teen social circuit. Veronica had met a bunch of idiots and ingrates.

"Did you have to say those things about our two countries?"

Veronica swiveled in her chair to face her mother. "He doesn't even know the history of his own government! I simply pointed out some facts about France and the United States."

"His father was offended."

Veronica threw up her hands. "Exactly! His silly son didn't even know that he should be offended. After all that, he asked me to go to a show tomorrow."

Interest flooded her mother's face. "What did you say?"

Veronica snorted. "No."

"But he's an attractive boy. And this would be a good alliance for your father. You can overlook his intellectual inferiority, surely."

"You can't be asking me to tolerate a dolt."

Her mother crossed her arms over her chest. "I've tolerated plenty of dolts."

"Father isn't a dolt. He's the most intelligent man I know."

"Contact the boy and tell him you changed your mind," her mother said. "Now, Veronica."

10

"My father has nothing to do with my work," Veronica said as they headed away from the safe house. She sat in the back seat as Campo drove. Harroway still had her gun and kept glancing back to check on her. She acted indifferent but continued to watch for the first opportunity to snatch it from him.

"I don't know if I believe that," he said.

Veronica hugged her arms across her ribcage. "You can believe it or not. The fact is that we don't speak about each other's work." Harroway wanted answers, Veronica knew. That was exactly why she regarded him warily and would until she figured a way out of this mess.

He glanced back at her and looked as if he might reply, but then turned and asked Campo, "Where are we going?"

"The question should be, what are we going to do with our guest?" said Campo. "I'm loathe to compromise the whereabouts of another of our safe houses."

Veronica's mouth felt like sandpaper. She fished around in her bag for a mint when Harroway noticed and reached back to grab her arm. "What are you doing?"

She tried to wrench her arm from his grasp. "What are you so nervous about? I'm looking for a mint. You already searched my purse and took my gun and phone."

"Why don't I find the mint for you?"

"I'm pretty sure I can take care of things without your help," Veronica said, pulling the purse closer. Just as she did this, she spotted a black sedan pull up alongside of them to the right and the driver's side window open. She saw a glint and yelled, "Gun!"

"Get down," shouted Harroway, who lowered his window and began firing at the gunman.

Veronica crouched down, wishing she had her weapon. She could at least keep them from being killed, rather than cowering in the back seat. Campo floored the SUV, and the car lurched forward. The gunfire soon stopped, and Veronica peered out the back window to see that the sedan had gotten stuck behind a large truck. "Give me my gun, and I can cover the rear," she said, but Harroway's attention was on their driver.

"You've been hit," he said to Campo, whose shoulder was soaked in blood. "Pull over. I'll drive." He pointed to a row of beach shops. "Behind those stores."

Veronica scooted back onto the seat while Campo headed toward the shops and stopped in an adjacent alleyway. Harroway hurried out and went around to help him into the passenger seat. The blood had soaked the front of his shirt and was spreading.

"We need to stop the bleeding," he said. "I wonder if the bullet is still in there?"

"Here, let me see," said Veronica.

Harroway appeared dubious.

"I've been shot myself," she said. He let her lean over the car seat. She eased Campo forward and pulled up his shirt to inspect the back of his shoulder. No exit wound. "The bullet is in there alright. It's going to need to come out so the wound can be stitched up to stop the bleeding."

Harroway hesitated, then said to Campo, "Helga's close. I'm taking you there. She's the only one I know who can help us."

"I can't," said Campo. "Call your doctor friend."

"We don't have a choice. I'm sorry but we're going there." Harroway's brow furrowed as Campo groaned and looked as if he might pass out. "Stay awake," he said as the man's head listed to one side. Then he turned back to Veronica and said, "Put pressure on the wound. I'm going to get him to someone who can help."

Harroway got behind the wheel and pulled out of the alleyway and headed back to Pacific Coast Highway while Veronica pressed firmly on the wound with a wad of napkins that Harroway found in the glove box. He kept glancing in the rearview mirror and then at Campo as he drove, a worried look on his face.

"How long have you worked together?" Veronica asked. "You seem to be quite familiar."

"That happens when you work with someone."

"Is he your official partner?"

"You ask a lot of questions."

"I'm just making conversation."

"You said you've been shot. When was that?" he asked her.

"Now who's asking too many questions?"

"I'm just making conversation."

Robert watched Veronica apply pressure to Campo's

wound and wondered what she was up to. She was clearly fishing, but for what? Information about his and Campo's operation? He glanced behind them for signs of the sedan and thankfully didn't see anyone. With all seemingly clear, he decided to make the call that Campo had asked him not to. He punched Helga's number into his cellphone. She answered on the first ring.

"Robbie?" she asked tentatively.

"It's me."

"If you're calling about Sassy, she's doing fine. How's the search going?"

"Not well, I'm afraid, and we've got another problem. Campo had an accident. I'm going to bring him to you. He needs a bullet removed."

Helga was silent for a moment, then she said quietly, "Of course, Robbie. I'll get things ready."

Robert hung up the phone and glanced at Veronica, who continued to apply pressure to the wound. "How long until we reach our destination?" she asked.

"About thirty minutes. How is the blood loss?"

"It seems to have slowed down." Campo lay back, quiet, eyes closed and breathing more evenly. Blood covered Veronica's hands, but she didn't seem to notice. She stayed helping him.

"So, when were you shot before?"

Veronica seemed to consider her response. "A few years back during an assignment. The coward shot me in the back."

"Someone wasn't playing fair," he said.

Veronica's voice took on a hard edge. "Human traffickers don't play fair, I've found. Especially with women."

"But you survived." He checked the rearview mirror for the highway patrol, then glanced at her.

I survived," she echoed, then turned her attention back to Campo.

49

11

*V*eronica tried, but she couldn't keep the thought of Horatio wanting her dead out of her head. True, there had been a mess to clean up with the last operation, and Horatio had been benched, but that wasn't entirely her fault. She stared at Campo's blood-soaked shirt and reminded herself that, in fact, the entire ordeal wasn't at all her fault.

"He wishes to see you."

Veronica shut off the faucet at the farm-style sink and dried her hands on the coarse fabric of her dress. Her skin crawled at the summons as she followed the woman down a darkened passageway until they came to what she knew to be the leader's main quarters. Once ushered inside, the door closed behind her. Veronica's stomach roiled at the sinister and darkly shrewd information she had uncovered about the man now sitting in a chair near the window. She wanted to look around and scope the place but kept her eyes in front of her. He stood and turned to her. "Sarah, how are your accommodations?" He walked toward her with a side-to-side gait, the musky, sweet scent of patchouli coming with him. His graying hair was a frizzy mass on his head, and a long, unkempt beard hung from his chin. As he came closer, she could smell the unwashed graying robe with white brocade that hung on his large frame.

Veronica cast her eyes to the floor in a forced portrayal of respect. "Fine, thank you."

He came to stand in front of her and lifted her chin with cold fingers. "No need to be shy, Sarah. And please call me Messiah Jacob. I'm sure your sponsor told you how to address me when in my presence."

"Yes, forgive me, Messiah Jacob. I'm still settling in." It took everything in Veronica to not turn her head from his smell and touch.

"Good," he said, letting go of her chin, his eyes sweeping the length of her body. "I see you are wearing the appropriate clothing."

She affected a shy smile and looked down at the heavy gray sack dress she wore, now splattered with water from washing the midday meal dishes.

"Has Shoshana told you of the ceremony tomorrow night?"

Veronica nodded. A warning of fear felt cold on the back of her neck. What if something went wrong and the ceremony went beyond her control? He could drug and rape her.

"Don't be afraid, my child. The ceremony is sanctioned by God. He has chosen me, his son, to oversee it." He put his hands on her shoulders, and his long nails scratched against the rough fabric of her dress. As he licked his full, red lips, his hooded eyes assessed everything around him. She looked down, averting her eyes from the bulge of his stomach against the dingy caftan. If there was a god, she was certain he wouldn't have picked this creep to be his messiah.

When the car headed into a wooded area in the Santa Monica Mountains, Veronica said, "I'm managing to keep the blood flow to as little as possible, but are we almost there?"

"Five minutes," said Harroway.

Soon after, they pulled up a gravel drive and crunched their way to a small cabin nestled in the forest. It looked like what Veronica imagined a gingerbread house would. As they parked and Harroway turned off the car, an older, heavyset woman wearing an apron advanced down the stairs towards them.

When Robert pulled into Helga's driveway, she was already waiting for them. He lowered the windows and let the car roll to a stop beneath the large oak tree that shaded the porch during the heat of summer. After he killed the engine, Helga leaned through the passenger window and laid a hand alongside Campo's cheek, then smoothed back his hair. Campo moaned and his eyes fluttered open, widening when they saw her face. Robert climbed out and took the opportunity to pull him from the car. With the help of Helga, they walked him to the steps. A gush of fresh blood began to seep through his shirt, his breathing becoming more labored from the effort.

"What is going on, Robbie?" Helga asked as they guided Campo up the steps and into the cabin. They dragged him the last few feet across the room and eased him down on the sofa and stretched him out. "And who is that woman in the car?"

"Long story, and I don't have all of the details, anyway. Let's just say, she's someone we need to keep an eye on."

Helga looked down at Campo. "This will do just fine. Nice and close to the kitchen." Then she met Robert's eyes. "I'm surprised he agreed to come here."

"He didn't want to come." Robert was honest. "But I had nowhere else to take him. I knew that you'd be able to help."

"That I can," she said, moving to the kitchen where she picked up a tray containing medical supplies, including a metal bowl, surgical tweezers, and a bottle of iodine.

"Can I do anything?"

"I've got this covered, but why don't you pop in and assure Sassy that all is well. I ordered her to stay in her room, and I'm sure she's confused by now. This is a painful process, so if there's screaming, tell her to pay no attention."

Robert hesitated, wondering what Veronica was up to, but then reminded himself that he had her gun and phone.

The second the cabin door closed, Veronica began searching the car. Campo had to have a weapon hidden in here somewhere. But all she found were candy wrappers and spectacles. Harroway had taken the car keys. She could hotwire the vehicle, but where would she go? She gave up and climbed into the back seat.

Just then, Harroway came out of the house and walked toward the car. He opened the back door and handed her a damp paper towel, then leaned on the frame. "I thought you might have escaped into the woods by now. Of course, you'd likely be attacked by a mountain lion when the sun sets, especially with fresh blood on your hands. Better to stay where you are."

"Look, Harroway, enough of this game." Veronica wiped Campo's blood off her hands and threw the paper towel on the ground.

He gave her an engaging smile as an answer and hung there, relaxed, while she tried to remind herself of exactly what she needed from both men.

"Certainly, we're on a first name basis by now. Call me Robert."

"Fine, Robert, may I have my phone and gun?"

They stared at each other in silence. Then he spoke. "Will you confirm with me that your assignment is me."

"Yes. The CIA wants to speak with you. You are a wanted man."

He pulled her phone out of his back pocket and handed it to her. "And it appears you are a wanted woman."

She grabbed the phone from his grasp and saw that it was dead. She turned it over and flipped the back open. "You took out the battery?"

"I won't have this location compromised by the people who obviously want you dead. Who would you be contacting anyway? Not your handler."

"No, but I do have someone to call who can sort through this whole mess."

"Your father?"

Veronica glared at him without responding.

"Your father has been indicted for treason."

eronica's expression went from disbelief to outrage as the news settled in. "That's impossible," she sputtered. "My father would never betray his country." She looked deeply shaken and as if she might cry. She shook her head, a look of defiance lighting her eyes on fire. "This is all a big mistake." She pulled her shoulders back and faced him. "I need to go to my father."

"Seeing your father is a terrible idea. For all you know, they've indicted him to smoke you out." Robert sighed. "You're not thinking clearly. And you could easily compromise me with all you've seen the last twenty-four hours. You need to stay put."

"So, you're keeping me hostage?"

"I prefer to think of you as my guest."

Veronica suddenly lunged toward him and slammed her palms against his chest, sending him stumbling backward. Robert regained his footing on the gravel drive as she reached for the gun in the back of his pants, but he stopped her, grabbing her by the wrists. Her eyes narrowed, and she struggled to pull her hands from his grasp. Just then the front door opened, and Helga stepped to the edge of the porch. "All okay out here, Robbie?" She wore her apron, but he knew she had her Walther pistol in its pocket.

"We were just leaving," Robert said as Veronica stopped squirming and he pulled her closer to him. "I'll check in with you soon."

Helga hesitated, then nodded and went back inside the cabin.

"My, my," said Veronica when the door shut. "If I didn't know any better, I'd say she's also an MI6 operative."

Robert stayed expressionless, still holding Veronica close. He knew there was no point in denying the obvious, but he wasn't going to let her dissect the reaction on his face. And truth be told, he found it rather exciting to be this near to her —even if she was technically the enemy.

Veronica stopped struggling and felt an involuntary shiver at being so near to Robert. "You can unhand me," she said, collecting herself. "I won't lunge for your gun. I promise."

He hesitated, then let her go. She continued to face him. Though she wished to use her phone to verify his story about her father, Robert was right to remove her battery. Veronica knew what it could mean if this location were breached. Any number of enemies could storm the cabin while he and the woman and Campo slept. Quite possibly set the cabin ablaze in the dry Southern California brush.

"I agree that me showing my face currently isn't prudent. I have my own safe house of sorts not too far from here. If you could drop me off there, you can go find whoever it is you're looking for."

A flicker of surprise crossed Robert's eyes. "And what tells you I am looking for someone?"

"It must be a missing person—someone important to you. Otherwise, you wouldn't keep checking your phone every few minutes."

"Where is your safe house?" Robert asked.

"Pacific Palisades."

Robert's eyebrows shot up. "Pricey area."

"It's a small place." Why was she defending herself to this man?

"Very well. Let's get going."

Veronica gave Robert directions, and they headed out of the mountains and back down Pacific Coast Highway. As they traveled, Veronica remained vigilant to ensure they weren't being followed. At the same time, Robert's words regarding her father ping-ponged in her head. She knew her father had to have enemies, given his trajectory. He had risen quickly in the ranks as a military attaché and even more quickly when he joined the DIA. Veronica suffered many snide remarks about being his daughter during her career, and how it was his influence that had led to what some considered plum assignments.

WHEN THEY ARRIVED at her condo complex, she directed Robert to park in her carport. He shut off the engine. When he didn't say anything, she suggested, "Perhaps we can call this even. We both know where the other is hiding when in LA."

"For all I know, you don't have a place here," he said. "And what about your assignment to detain me?"

"I have no idea what to do about that assignment, given that the man who ordered me to proceed may want me dead. And that would make no sense to have you drive me all the way here so I can make a break for it the minute you park. I could have jumped out when the traffic slowed." She threw up her hands. "Would you like to come in?"

"Serving your country is the highest honor you can possibly garner," said her father to Veronica the day she became a CIA agent. He had summoned her to his office, where he pulled out a bottle of scotch and poured them both a glass. Her heart filling with more pride than she had ever felt, she sat on the edge of the seat across from her father and reached for the glass of amber liquid. Holding the glass tight, she waited as he continued to speak.

"I know that I was skeptical when you chose to be an agent, but I will admit you have surpassed my expectations," her father said, his deep voice low and measured. He wore the brown cardigan he often donned while working at home. The smell of tobacco from his pipe lingered in the air. "You have taken on the very important task of safeguarding our nation from security threats. I know that may put you in the path of danger, and I can see now," he paused as if to assess her, "you are ready for that task."

Veronica's head buzzing with his words, she raised her scotch as he said, "To justice, honor, and love of country."

Then they clinked glasses, and he gave her a rare smile before taking a drink. Veronica wanted to promise that she would always make him proud. Instead, she nodded and drank the scotch, unable to speak as its heat trailed down her throat and into her belly.

13

*T*hey made their way along a pathway lined with blue-headed stalks of agapanthus, bright pink impatiens, and begonias. Robert glanced around them as they walked, his hand resting on the handle of his gun. The sound of splashing from the nearby pool echoed as Veronica slid a key into her front door lock.

"It's small but serves my purposes," she said as she opened the door. She motioned for Robert to enter.

He walked into the living room with its beige walls, the color of sand. The furniture was contemporary—couch, coffee table, two chairs, all white—the only splash of color in the room a patterned red rug. The white made the room seem breezy and open, the rug welcoming. A black metal floor lamp arched over one end of the couch. Veronica went into the open kitchen and laid her purse on the bar counter. To the left, a short hallway went to a back bedroom, its door open. A sliding glass door took up much of the wall opposite the front door and led to a small balcony. "Do you mind?" Robert said as he unlocked and slid the door open. He looked over the neighboring rooftops to see the sun setting into the ocean.

Robert turned to watch Veronica in the kitchen. She had removed her heels and stood barefoot, examining the contents of her refrigerator. Pulling out a bottle of wine, she set it on the kitchen bar island.

"Would you like something to drink before you go?" she asked him.

"I wouldn't say no to a glass of chilled wine," Robert said, walking to the island to face her. She returned his gaze, and he thought she must be tired and feeling, perhaps, defeated. "What will you do about the news of your father?"

She didn't answer, but poured a full glass of wine, and then another, handing one to him. Then she drank a generous amount of her glass and set it back on the counter. "I haven't a clue."

Robert swirled the wine in his glass, put his nose in to sniff the aromas, then took a drink. His gut clenched at thoughts of Fiona missing. He hadn't heard anything from his sources about where she might be.

Veronica picked up the bottle and motioned with it to the balcony. "I find the answers sometimes come when I sit outside. That or I finish the bottle of wine and forget the questions."

Robert smiled. "After you."

She dusted off a chair and Robert did the same. The moist ocean air lifted with a breeze to where they sat beside a small metal table. Robert took a drink and sighed. "I have to say the view is worth every penny you pay here," he said.

Veronica took a sip of wine. "This is one of my favorite spots. No one knows about this place. Not even my..." She trailed off.

"Father?" Robert finished her sentence. "So, your own private refuge."

She took another drink of the wine. Without looking at him, she said, "You know my trouble. Tell me yours. What will you do about the person you're searching for? I'm curious." After a few silent moments, she turned to look at him, her blue eyes waiting.

Robert knew that he should keep his defenses up, but somehow here in this neutral space, he felt like he could trust Veronica. He took a deep breath and replied, "My sister."

Veronica pulled loose the bow at the neck of her blouse, then undid several buttons. She turned toward Robert, appearing surprised at his answer, her blouse falling open just enough to expose the tops of her full, soft breasts. Robert gave them an appreciative glance.

"So, we both have family troubles." She poured herself another glass of wine and held the bottle up. "More?"

Robert drained his glass and held it out. "Are we going for forgetting?"

Veronica clutched her wineglass by the stem and shook her head. "Never in a million years would I have thought that my father's name and the word treason could be uttered in the same breath. Unfortunately, that's not something I can forget. Your sister. Has she disappeared before?"

"Not since she had my niece seven years ago."

"I heard a little girl's voice when I was in your trunk. Was that her?"

"Yes, her name is Sally Ann. I call her Sassy for short."

Veronica turned to face him. "I have a proposal for you."

"Go on," said Robert.

"It seems I can't safely ask around about my father, and you've likely exhausted your resources with your sister. What if we check for each other? See if we can get somewhere?"

That wasn't a bad idea, thought Robert. "How do I know you'll hold up your end of the bargain?"

"I could say the same about you," she said.

Robert gazed out at the setting sun and thought, any lead about Fiona would be better than nothing. "It's a deal," he said, lifting his glass.

Veronica smiled one of her rare smiles and clinked his glass. "To answers. The sooner, the better. I have a secure phone line and computer network here if you'd like to use it."

"Let's get started."

Veronica felt a bit loosened up by the wine. When Robert stood, his body casting a shadow over her against the setting sun, she looked up at him and was once again struck by his virility. Very few men ever turned her head, and even fewer made her feel like running her fingers through their hair. He reached down for her hand and helped her to her feet, sending lightning bolts to the tips of her toes. For a moment, they stood suspended, inches from one another. Veronica thought he might kiss her, but then he broke the spell and said, "I'll take the computer."

Reining herself in, Veronica walked back into the living room and shut the sliding glass door. "I'll make some calls about your sister. But I need some more details." Then she deposited the bottle and her glass in the kitchen and walked back toward the bedroom as Robert followed her.

When they entered the room, Veronica noticed she hadn't made her bed the last time she was here. The sheets lay in a tangle, her nightgown flung across the pillow. She felt self-conscious with Robert in her personal space and went over and pulled up the duvet. Then she opened a rolltop desk that sat against the wall and pulled up the screen on her laptop. Robert hung back while she put in her passwords. She picked up a notepad and pencil. "Your sister's full name and date of birth?"

"Fiona Elaine Cartwright. Born May 27, 1979."

"She has a different last name. Is that her married name?"

"No, we're half-siblings. Same mother. Different father."

"Where was she last seen?"

"Santa Monica, at her home there."

"Known associates who could possibly factor into this?"

Robert hesitated. Finally, he answered. "Jimmy Shivers."

Certainly, she'd heard him wrong. "Not *the* Jimmy Shivers. Scotland's dangerous crime lord?"

Robert put his head in his hands and gazed at the floor. "He's Sassy's father."

14

"*I*'m sure you've considered that Shivers may have your sister?" said Veronica.

"If he did, I would have received a demand of some sort," said Robert. "Nothing has come. He's not a very nice man, and that's putting it mildly."

Veronica tapped her pencil on the notepad. "Does Shivers know about Sassy?"

"I'm not sure. My sister never shared that fact with me." He pushed away any thought of Sassy being in danger.

Veronica began drawing circles on the notepad. "You're not sure because your sister won't tell you, or because you didn't want to question her?"

"Fiona tries not to worry me and said she left him before she was showing, but I've always wondered what he knows."

"Men like Shivers are very controlling. They don't like letting go of what or who they believe belongs to them. I would be suspicious enough to believe he has kept tabs on your sister. Let me make a couple calls."

"I'll get to work then," said Robert, troubled by the truth of Veronica's words. There wasn't a time that he didn't worry for his sister. He sat down at the computer and logged onto the MI6 database. After some digging, he found that there wasn't much on Gerard Valencia, but what Robert did see portrayed a man who stuck to the rules. He'd gathered enemies along the way with his insistence on going by the book. Given what Robert was seeing, it could be that his arrest was a frame-up, as Veronica insisted.

Veronica called her source at the FBI. Shayla Foster picked up on the first ring. "V.V., I'm so glad to finally hear from you."

"I'm sure you've heard about my father?" Veronica asked, her stomach sinking at the thought of her proud father in a jail cell.

"Yes, how are you holding up?"

Veronica began scribbling on the notepad vigorously. "I'm holding up."

"I've tried to keep tabs on any information I might be able to share with you," Shayla said. "Trust me, I have both ears open."

Veronica gulped. Shayla's comment about having something she might be able to share meant the FBI had something on her father. Although, one thing Veronica knew for certain, if Shayla heard truly shattering news about him, she would find a way to get it to her.

"I'm calling about a missing person. It's unrelated."

She heard relief in Shayla's voice when she replied, "Let me see if I can help you. What's the name?"

Veronica gave her the information.

"It'll take a bit of digging, but I'll see what I can find. You sure you're okay? That last assignment with the cult, and now this."

Veronica glanced at Robert, busily tapping away, absorbed by whatever he was researching on the computer. "I'll be okay, but thanks for asking."

"Call if you need to talk," said Shayla. "You know I'm good at listening." Veronica knew that to be true. She and Shayla had met in France when their fathers were working in the US embassy there. Both had been shy teens who became fast friends.

Veronica hung up and dialed another source.

An hour later, Robert closed the computer as Veronica hung up from a call.

"Anything?" she asked. He could tell she was trying to hide the hopefulness in her voice.

"Your father looks to be the outstanding man you describe him to be," said Robert. "Which means he's either very good at hiding his tracks, or he has found himself in the middle of a massive frame-up. How about you?"

"The sources I spoke to weren't able to find any word on your sister. But I have someone at the FBI who is a topnotch sleuth. If there's something there, she's going to find it. I hope to hear from her by morning." Veronica yawned.

"It's late," said Robert. He stretched his back and raised arms over his head.

Veronica nodded. "I'm still wearing the same clothes and

would love a good, hot shower." She looked thoughtful for a minute. "Listen, I'll make you a deal."

Robert waited.

"You can stay here for the night, if you give me my gun back."

"And what if I don't stay? I take your gun with me?" He smiled, enjoying the spark in her eyes at his comment. She began to open her mouth to protest, but Robert held up his hand and said, "I'll be right back." He went into the living room and removed her gun and phone battery from his bag, then returned to the bedroom and handed them to her. "The safety is on."

She eyed the gun and asked, "Have you ever played Russian Roulette?"

"I can't say that I have," he said, slightly wary and curious where she was going with this. "Have you?"

Veronica turned the gun over in her hand. "No, but I've often thought how my work feels like I imagine Russian Roulette would."

Her comment hung in the air for a moment, then Robert cleared his throat. "I feel that way about my work sometimes. I guess the question is, why do we do it?"

Veronica put her gun in her bedside table. "That's something I ask myself quite often. I'll get you a blanket and a pillow for the couch."

AT SOME POINT in the night, a sound woke Robert. He listened, ready to reach for his gun, when he saw Veronica in the kitchen. She turned the water on and began to wash the dishes. He soon noticed that she continued to wash the same glass as the water streamed down the drain. After several minutes, he got up and went into the kitchen. As he drew closer, he heard what sounded like mumbling. He stood back as he strained to listen but couldn't make out the words. Could she be asleep? Then she laid the glass on the bottom of the sink. As he started to speak, she reached toward a magnetic knife holder on the wall and pulled down a large butcher knife. He moved toward her as she turned, eyes leaden, the knife grasped in her hand. "Come any closer, and I'll use this. I know the Messiah sent you."

"I'm not going to hurt you," he said in a low voice. "Just give me the knife."

She shook her head and waved it in front of him.

"It's me, Robert," he said in a soothing tone. "Hand me the knife now." He reached out his hand slowly.

Veronica suddenly got a confused look on her face, which gave him the opportunity to reach forward and grab the knife handle and yank it from her grasp. He set it behind him on the counter and advanced toward her cautiously. "It's me, Robert," he repeated.

Veronica blinked a few times, then shook her head, recognition dawning. "Robert?" She glanced around the kitchen and down at her nightgown, then back into his eyes. "What's going on?"

"You were sleepwalking."

"Dammit," she said, reaching over and turning off the faucet. Her eyes fell on the knife.

"Did I...?" She trailed off, trepidation in her eyes.

"Try to hurt me with the knife, no. But you were waving it around and talking about a messiah."

Veronica's face crumpled. She leaned her arms on the counter. "You know those assignments that stick with you? Won't leave you?" she nearly whispered.

"Quite well," Robert answered.

"What do you do to get them out of your head?"

Robert thought about his answer for a moment. "A stiff

drink, but that doesn't really help. What does is talking about it."

Veronica stood up. "I'm sorry I woke you. I'll see you in the morning." Then she walked back to her room and shut the door.

15

*V*eronica leaned against the door, taking long, slow breaths to center herself. She'd been on many missions, but none as unsettling as the last. Usually, she could push the images out of her head, but this time was different. She thought about Robert's offer to talk about what happened, and she felt a twinge of what? Regret? That she couldn't bring herself to even speak out loud about that final night at the compound? She had to admit the thought of divulging the sordid details would be a welcome relief, but she and Robert were spies. Trained to gather information. She'd learned from experience that anything she said could and probably would be used against her.

Back in bed, Veronica lay staring at the ceiling. She tried willing the thoughts of the assignment away but in the quiet night it was impossible.

"The Messiah is not happy with your progress."

Veronica turned from the sink to address her sponsor, a girl of eighteen, who was starting to show her pregnancy under the sack dress they each wore. "I'm just getting used to how things are done here."

The girl, who the Messiah had renamed Shoshana, held Veronica by the shoulders, anxiety flitting across her eyes. She looked toward the doorway and back at Veronica. "You have been honored with a request to participate in tonight's ceremony," Shoshana said. "You must understand the importance of this being given to you. To refuse would come with serious penalty." Her voice lowered with urgency. "I'm concerned for you."

Veronica stiffened involuntarily as Shoshana's eyes pleaded with her. She wanted to ask her what the penalty would be, but instead thought she'd make certain it didn't come to that.

"I'll participate," Veronica assured her, hoping to dispel the girl's fears. She didn't want to make the Messiah suspicious by seeming reluctant to take part.

Shoshana visibly relaxed. She turned and left the room, returning momentarily with a red gauze gown. "Put this on before the ceremony." She handed it to Veronica. "It is a holy gown." Her words held a devout commitment.

Veronica awoke in the early morning thinking of her father's predicament. Then she thought of her mother. She wished she could call her, but the CIA would be monitoring all communication. Plus, the last time they spoke, it ended in terse words, as it often did. She got out of bed and went to the closet, where she pulled out a short white robe and put it on over her nightgown.

In the kitchen, she found Robert opening cupboards. His black hair was out of its band and brushed his bare shoulders. She felt a warm rush when she eyed his smooth, well-sculpted chest.

"Good morning," he said. "I'm checking for coffee, or tea will do."

"I've got both." She moved into the kitchen to stand next to him. Reaching across him, she opened the cupboard to his right and grazed his chest. The contact sent sparks up and down her arm.

"Thanks," he said, reaching up for a bag of coffee. He set it on the counter next to the coffeemaker. He made no move to distance himself, and Veronica felt as if she was caught in an energy field. As if he was a magnet and she was metal.

Everything in Robert wanted to kiss Veronica. It was as if her lips, soft and rosy from sleep, invited him. As he had these thoughts, she moved distractingly close to pour water into the coffeemaker.

"You're a beautiful woman," he said in a throaty tone, feeling slightly overcome. He watched her face closely for a reaction.

A small smile turned up the edge of her mouth, and she looked up at him, eyes wide. "Thank you."

"If we weren't adversaries, I would ask if I could kiss you," he said.

"At the moment, we appear to be on the same side," she replied, tilting her face up.

Robert pulled Veronica to him and took her lips with his. As their mouths met, Veronica leaned back against the counter. They shared long, hungry kisses, then he opened her robe and unbuttoned her nightgown. When he placed the warmth of his mouth and then tongue on her soft breast, she stiffened and suddenly pulled her robe around herself. Backing up, he regained his composure, his breathing heavy.

Veronica's face became a solid mask, detached and unemotional as she tied the robe and wiped her lips with the back of her hand.

"I apologize. I shouldn't have," Robert said.

"No need to apologize." She turned and began to scoop coffee into the paper filter. "I just think it's best we don't make this more complicated than it already is." When she'd finished, she pulled her robe tighter around her and watched the coffee percolate.

Robert admonished himself for misinterpreting Veronica's messages. He never let his hormones get the better of him when he was working, and it now seemed he had moved forward on his desires alone.

Veronica's lips burned as she stood there. She felt frozen, not trusting herself. The pull between her and Robert was undeniable. But it was vital she keep her head on straight. Her and her father's life depended on it.

The phone in the bedroom rang, breaking the spell. "That may be news," she called over her shoulder as she headed to answer it.

"Yes?" Veronica said, relieved to no longer be seeing the look of hurt on Robert's face.

"It's Shayla. I've got some information about the missing woman, and there's something else you need to know."

Veronica could tell by the tone in her friend's voice that the something else wasn't good. She sat on the edge of her bed. "Is the something else about my family member?"

"Actually, it's about you," said Shayla.

Horatio flashed through Veronica's mind. "Go on."

"First, let me give you the info on Fiona Cartwright."

While Robert stood in the doorway, Veronica pulled out a notepad and pencil from her bedside table. "I'm ready."

"I went to where Cartwright's cellphone last pinged. It looks like the south of France."

Veronica looked toward Robert and addressed him. "Does the south of France mean anything?"

"Yes. Is Fiona there?"

"It looks that way." Veronica turned her attention back to Shayla. "Anything else, Shay?" Veronica heard voices on the other end of the phone, then static. "You still there?" The line went dead.

16

*V*eronica tried to ring Shayla back, but the call went straight to voicemail.

"No answer?"

Veronica shook her head.

"Fiona is in France?"

"She said south of France. The call was cut off before I could get more specifics. Any information for me?" Veronica looked toward the computer.

Robert went to the desk and sat down, then pulled up the MI6 database. He scrolled through the files until he came to one and clicked on it. "I've found a photo in our surveillance."

Veronica came to stand behind him. "My father?"

"It appears so." Robert clicked on the photo. There was her father with a woman.

"I don't recognize her. Does the file say who she is?"

"It does."

"Well, who is she?"

Robert swiveled around to look at her. "Are you sure you want to know?"

"Of course, I want to know," she said, putting her hands on her hips. "What kind of question is that?"

"Anya Sokolov. She's a Russian emissary focused on diplomatic relations between Russia and North America."

Veronica suddenly felt lightheaded. "I'm sure there's an explanation," she sputtered. "He was an attaché."

Robert turned back to the screen.

Veronica steadied herself on the back of the desk chair. "Can you enlarge the photo?" she asked, leaning over his shoulder to examine the picture of the two more closely. The woman was striking, with blond hair and aquiline features. She looked to be about Veronica's age, if not younger. Her father wore a black overcoat and was smiling, his hands clasped over the woman's. They stood next to a body of water.

"It looks like the photo is recent," Veronica murmured, her eyes locked on her father's face. Since when did he smile like that?

Robert was surprised at the photo. Nothing in Valencia's records had indicated a connection between him and the Russians. He snuck a glance at Veronica. Her face showed a cocktail of confusion, disbelief, and anger.

Robert typed onto the keyboard. "I have the location where this was taken," he said, turning to face her.

Veronica's eyes met his, and he saw hesitation in them.

"They were in Valencia, Spain," he continued, overlooking the Balearic Sea. "Your father is Spanish?"

"Half, yes. His father was Spanish and his mother American."

"Well, it appears the photo was taken just a few days ago, before your father's arrest."

Veronica started pacing in the middle of the room. "I've got to get to Spain."

"Someone is after you, Veronica."

"This is a solid lead regarding my father." Veronica began pulling open drawers and taking out clothing.

"Let's go together," he said.

The announcement caused Veronica to stop packing. "To Spain?"

"And France. We'll have better luck if we have each other's backs." He waited for her reply.

Veronica thought about his suggestion. Was he being serious? "How do I know I can trust you?" she asked.

"I could ask the same about you. This all started with you coming to get me, at the behest of your handler. I should be the one who is skittish, but for some reason, I'm not." Robert came to stand in front of her, and she stood motionless, feeling aroused, needing to step away from him.

"What is it they say, keep your friends close, but your enemies closer?" he said.

Veronica felt her heart quicken as Robert continued to stand near her. She tried to clear her head and weighed her options, which were pretty much nonexistent. "Okay," she finally said. "Let's go to Europe."

"I can book our flights," he said.

Veronica still felt hesitant. Everything was moving so fast. "Don't you need to check in with your handler?" she asked him.

"I have a few days off to find Fiona," he said.

Veronica nodded and went to sit down at the computer. "I need to check my texts. They're forwarded to my email," she assured him, "so I don't have to turn on my phone." She began scanning her emails. Several texts had come in from Horatio asking for status updates. The last text was—*V??? The brass is concerned*—early that morning. "I bet they are," she muttered. A message from her mother caught her eye: *I need to speak to you immediately. It's about your father.* She tapped one finger on the desk when an email suddenly popped up. The subject line made her heart ping. *Critical information about your father.* She didn't recognize the sender. She sat there for some moments, her finger hovering over the enter key.

She sensed Robert looking over her shoulder. "Are you going to open it?" he asked.

"It could just be spam."

"And it could give us some vital information," he replied in a low voice.

Somehow the two-letter word, us, gave Veronica courage. She took a breath and hit enter.

The email that opened included the photo they had just seen of her father and the Russian woman. Underneath in big, bold letters was a word that made her gasp. *TRAITOR.*

17

"*V*, get up and get ready for school. You're going to be late." Already dressed for the day in tailored gray pants and a pristine white shirt, her mother stood in Veronica's doorway. It was the morning after her fourteenth birthday.

Veronica stared at the ceiling. Her father had promised to come to her party but at the last moment said he was unable to get home in time. And Veronica had worked so hard to have a party her father would find acceptable. She had even endured the French ambassador's son ogling her all night.

"V, please, no more moping," her mother said. When Veronica didn't move, her mother entered the room, the sound of her gold bracelet tinkling against her watch as she came to stand by her bed. Then she surprised Veronica by sitting down next to her. "I know it's difficult to not have your father here. Especially on important occasions."

She had expected a scolding, but her mother's tone was soft. Veronica sat up in bed, her back against the headboard.

"My father, as you know, was also a powerful man. Even

before he was bank president, I rarely saw him. I wasn't even sure if he would walk me down the aisle at my wedding."

Her mother rarely spoke about herself. Especially her earlier years. Veronica wanted her to continue, to stay seated beside her. "What was your wedding day like?"

Her mother flashed a faraway smile. "It was lovely. Your father looked so handsome in his uniform. The church was filled with masses of beautiful flowers and glowing candles."

Were her mother's eyes misting? This was a side Veronica hadn't seen before. "Was it the most perfect day you ever imagined? Were you very happy?" asked Veronica, envisioning her mother in a big white dress with her father at the altar.

Her mother placed a hand on Veronica's arm. "It was the perfect day. And you have many wonderful days in front of you. With luck, your father will be at your next birthday." She stood then. "Do get up. The driver is waiting."

Veronica was about to erase the incriminating email of her father, but Robert stopped her. "Don't. We might be able to trace it to the sender."

"It's unlikely the person used an identifiable IP address," she said.

"The email is also evidence."

Veronica slapped her hands on her thighs. "What I need is answers."

"And we're going to get them. We just need time and a

little luck...." His voice trailed off. "What name should I register you under?"

Veronica went to her closet and got down on her knees to pull up a corner of the carpeting, exposing a floor safe. She dialed in the combination and pulled it open. Then she extracted a pile of passports and brought them to the desk.

Robert stared at the numerous passports, a shocked expression on his face. "I thought I had a lot of aliases. He opened the first one on the stack. "Hazel Gerard. Interesting choice using your father's first name as your last." He opened another passport and smiled. "I like her." He held up the photo of Veronica as a blond. She had a smirk on her face.

"Delia Swan," said Veronica. "She'll do." She took the passport from his hand and checked the last time she'd used it. A date stamp for Ireland. Sweden before that. Though it was just last year, it felt like a lifetime ago. "I've got some hair dye in the bathroom."

When Veronica closed the door, Robert dialed Helga's number.

"How is he?" Robert asked.

"I was able to remove the bullet and stitch him up. Gave him something for the pain and to ward off infection. He's asleep now."

Robert was relieved he didn't have to face his uncle just yet about taking him to Helga.

"I'm going to take the phone outside with me," Helga said, her voice a whisper. He heard her footsteps cross the cabin, then the front door open and close. "I'm away from prying ears," she said.

"Speaking of, how is Sassy?"

"Keeping herself busy. I have her drawing a get-well card now."

"Good. Thank you, Helga. For everything," Robert said.

"I'm always here for you, you know that. To answer your question, your uncle's head is as hard as a boulder, but we had some words."

Robert was almost afraid to ask. "Good words?"

"Don't you worry yourself about that. You've got more important things to tend to. Tell me, are you still with the woman you had in tow?"

"Yes."

"I might be an old woman, but I have eyes. That's a she-cat you've got there."

"It's strictly business. We're helping each other out."

Helga laughed, her tone full of mirth. "Robbie, I had a hand in raising you. I know when you've got eyes for a lass."

"Well, my focus right now is on finding Fiona."

Helga's voice sobered up. "Any word?"

"Yes. I'll be getting on a flight to the south of France in a few hours. Her cellphone targeted her there."

"Oh, my," Helga said.

"Maybe it's just a coincidence."

"You know I don't believe in coincidences," she said.

"Neither do I."

Veronica waited in the bathroom for the hair dye to do its

work. She wasn't about to leave the room with a plastic bag on her head. The next time Robert saw her it would be as a blond. As she sat, she heard his voice in the other room talking on the phone. She couldn't make out what he was saying, but there was an easiness and warmth to his tone. He laughed suddenly, and she felt a twinge of envy toward whoever was on the other end of the line.

Veronica rinsed out the dye, then took out the blow dryer and dried her new hair into submission. She surveyed herself in the mirror and smiled. It was always fun to take on a new look. After sliding on lipstick and eyeliner, she emerged from the bathroom to find Robert at the computer. He looked up when she came out, his eyes lighting up with undisguised pleasure. "I like you as a blond."

Veronica smiled, a rush of pleasure washing through her at his approval. She was about to answer him when there was a sound in the front room. Within seconds, she had her gun out of the bedside table, and Robert had his in hand.

"I'll go first," he mouthed, pointing to the hallway. Veronica knew that meant she would cover him. She followed a few feet behind, her gun extended. When he went around the corner at the end of the hallway, a shot rang out, then she heard a groan and a thud. Holding her breath, lest she miss the telltale sound of someone pulling the trigger, she sprang out from the hallway ready to fire. Relief flooded through her when she saw Robert standing over the body of the assassin who had been after her since the safe house at the beach. She'd recognize that pockmarked face anywhere.

18

"*T*hat's the man who came after me," said Veronica. The assassin lay on his back, dead, a bullet in his chest. Blood had started to seep onto the carpeting. Suddenly, sirens sounded in the distance.

"Someone must have called the police," Robert said. "We need to get out of here."

Veronica ran to her room and pulled open the safe, then grabbed a bag containing clothing and toiletries from the top shelf and threw everything from the safe into it. Next, she ran to the desk and removed a manila envelope and a roll of stamps. She grabbed her purse.

"I've got the computer and my bag," said Robert. "Anything else?"

The sound of sirens grew louder. "We don't have time to wipe the place down. Let's go." Veronica raced outside, Robert at her heels.

When they got to the car, Robert slammed it into gear and backed out. As they headed for the exit, sirens blared. "Get down," he said.

Veronica ducked as lights flashed and squad cars

screeched in while they casually drove out. She stayed low for a time, watching him check the rearview mirror as he drove. "Anything?"

"I think we're good."

Veronica sat up and smoothed her hair. "I want to know how the assassin found out about this place," she said.

Robert made a right and headed down Interstate 1. "An excellent question we can ponder on our flight to France," he said. "The plane leaves in three hours. We should be at LAX in about twenty minutes."

"You know your way around LA," Veronica commented.

"I've spent quite a bit of time here."

"Your sister lives here?"

Robert nodded, and his brow furrowed. She'd come to recognize that look. Suddenly, she felt a wave of compassion for him. She reached out and put her hand on his forearm. "We'll find her," she said quietly.

Veronica's touch was so gentle and reassuring, Robert felt a warm glow in his chest. He glanced at her and tried to make eye contact, but she pulled her hand away and turned to look out the passenger side window. Robert thought he'd known complicated women, but he was beginning to think he'd met his match with Veronica.

As they drove through afternoon traffic, Veronica pulled out a manila envelope and wrote an address on the front. Then she took her other passports out of her travel bag and put them in the envelope, sealed and stamped it.

"There's a post office up on the right," she said. "If you just pull through the drive, we can drop this in."

"Good thinking," said Robert. "It would have been hard to explain all of those passports to security. Who are you mailing them to?"

"My mother. She'll know what to do with them."

"You haven't spoken much about her," said Robert as he drove into the post office parking lot. Veronica handed him the envelope, and he slipped it into the box and then steered the car back onto the street.

"There's not that much to say," said Veronica. "In many ways, my mother has lived all these years in my father's shadow."

"Have you talked to her since your father went into custody?"

Veronica shifted in her seat. "No, I will." She looked back out the window, ending the conversation.

When they arrived at LAX, Robert parked his uncle's car in long-term parking, then grabbed their bags. A plane flew overhead, and the smell of jet fuel hung in the air. "We need to head to Air France," he said, picking up his pace. "We can get our weapons through if I use my MI6 credentials and claim the guns as mine."

When they got to a crosswalk and waited for the light to change, Veronica asked, "As for our story, I'm what, your companion?"

Robert grinned. "I like the sound of that." Did he see a smile tugging at the sides of her mouth?

They passed through security without incident. While waiting to board at the Air France terminal, Robert checked his phone for any breaking news about the shooting. Nothing yet.

"Maybe give your FBI friend a call before we board to see if she has any new information," he suggested. "The phone will ping here, but there are so many flights going out that it will be difficult for them to determine where you're going."

Veronica pulled her phone out of her bag and powered it on, then pressed a number. He watched as she waited, noting how stylish she was in sleek black leather pants, boots, and a green blouse. How her hair fell over one shoulder when she leaned down. Her movements quick and decisive. Then he reminded himself his job was to stay focused on Fiona.

Robert's idea to phone Shayla was a good one. Better to get any information she could now when it would be difficult to trace where she was heading.

"V. V., there you are. I'm sorry we got cut off before." Her friend sounded relieved, but Veronica also noted an awkward tone to her voice.

"You were about to tell me something," Veronica said.

Shayla was quiet on the other end.

"Please, Shay."

"I can't talk right now," said Shayla. "I'm in the middle of something."

Veronica ran her tongue over her lips. "That night in the pool at the embassy when we were thirteen. The boy you liked, what was his name?"

She heard Shayla take a quick breath. "Reginald. His father worked for the Russian Embassy, or was it the Spanish Embassy?"

"I was thinking about that night recently. How much fun we had," said Veronica. "Perhaps we can revisit it when I see you again. I'll be in touch."

Veronica was about to hang up when she heard Shayla say, "Wait, V.V., you still there?"

"Yes."

"Be careful."

Veronica's shoulders slouched in frustration, then she hung up the phone.

"Anything?" Robert asked. He had gone to a nearby sundries stand while she was talking and bought a pack of gum. He offered her some.

She pulled out a piece and unwrapped it, sticking it in her mouth. After she had chewed for a short time, she replied, "My friend wasn't able to tell me much. The call was being monitored. She mentioned the Spanish and Russian embassies, so a confirmation of what we already know."

Veronica put her phone on the floor and crushed it with her foot as they announced boarding for their flight. She picked up the remnants. "I wish I had time to deposit this in another terminal."

Robert held out his hand. "Give it to me."

Phone in hand, he took long strides to a bathroom across the way. He walked toward a janitor's cart that sat out front, slipping the phone into the trash as he passed and went inside. Soon after, he emerged, a smile on his face.

As Robert headed toward her, Veronica realized that for the first time since this horrible ordeal had started, she felt hopeful that things might just work out after all.

19

*W*hen the flight took off after waiting in line to be directed onto the tarmac, Robert finally relaxed. He glanced over at Veronica, who checked out the drink menu several times as the plane leveled off. He thought about making conversation when the flight attendant announced that the journey to Toulouse-Blagnac Airport would take fourteen and a half hours.

Veronica turned to him. "It'll be 5 pm when we land in France tomorrow."

Robert nodded as Veronica reached for the inflight magazine and pulled it out of the seat back pocket. She began absently flipping through the pages. "I can't tell you how many of these I've looked at," she said. "We moved often when I was young. Too many overseas flights to count."

"Did you enjoy it?" Robert asked.

She thought a moment. "To be honest, it was difficult. Having to make new friends again and again was exhausting." She slapped the magazine shut and looked uncomfortable at having revealed this about herself.

"That would be exhausting," he agreed.

"What about you? Where did you grow up?" She returned the magazine to the back of the seat.

"In the south of France and England, primarily."

"How did you get involved in the work?" she asked.

Robert shifted in his seat.

"Never mind," she said. "I'm prying."

The steward appeared then, a tray held aloft. "Can I get you anything to drink? We'll be serving dinner in about an hour."

"I'd like a beer and a water," said Robert. The steward nodded and directed his attention to Veronica.

"Please give me a chardonnay and a water."

After he left, Robert said, "You've probably figured out that Campo has had a great influence on me. It was his idea for me to sign up."

Veronica nodded. "He seems to have your best interest at heart."

"I owe him for that," said Robert, "and much more. I never knew my father, and my mother..." he trailed off, then cleared his throat and continued, "had her problems, let's say. Campo was always there for me."

Robert took a sip of his beer and pushed a button on the television screen in front of him. Part of Veronica wanted to continue probing to find out more about his relationship with Campo. But the other part of her wanted to stop asking questions and try to enjoy the flight and reprieve from immediate danger. In the silence between them, though, her thoughts quickly turned to her father's situation. She tried to picture him sitting in a jail cell and found it impossible to do so. How could she have missed even a small sign of something so dire as her father committing treason? Then again, how well did she really know her father? She was beginning to think not as well as she thought.

It was late afternoon on a drizzly Friday, and Veronica stood ringing the bell at the front door of her parents' brownstone in Georgetown.

Their maid, Leticia, answered, her eyes lighting up. "Miss Veronica," she said, pulling the door open and taking her umbrella. "Your mother isn't here, but your father is in his study."

Veronica hung her raincoat on a peg in the entryway next to the bucket with her umbrella. "Thank you so much, Leticia." She walked down the carpeted hallway, the grandfather clock's ticking the only sound. Stopping at the study door, she knocked gently.

"Yes," her father called out.

"It's me."

"Come in."

When she walked in, her father looked up from his desk and removed his reading glasses. He had a document in front of him that he slipped into a file folder.

"This is a surprise," he said, motioning for her to take a seat across from him.

Veronica set her purse on the floor and sat, enjoying as always, the feel of the butter- smooth leather.

"I'd heard you got back from the last assignment," he said.

A wave of anxiety washed through Veronica at the mention of the mission at the cult compound. A couple of beats, and she replied, keeping her voice steady, "I was at headquarters and thought I'd stop in and say hello. I hope I'm not interrupting something."

Her father cleared his throat. "I know we can't talk directly about your recent assignment, but are you alright?" He studied her face.

Veronica was momentarily taken aback by his question. Her father had never asked her how she was holding up following a mission. She straightened her back. "I'm fine. Business as usual. The mission had a few hiccups but was ultimately deemed a success. Or so I'm told."

Her father reached for his pipe and checked that it held tobacco, then took his brass lighter and lit it. Leaning back in his leather chair, he appeared thoughtful. "I don't know if we could call that last mission business as usual. From the reports that have crossed my desk, I'd say it was quite unusual." He took a puff of the pipe, and the smoke created a circular pattern in the air.

All this talk about the mission was bringing back images, and Veronica suddenly felt like getting some air. "Excuse me for a moment. I need to use the powder room."

Her father nodded.

Veronica went to the bathroom down the hall, locked the door behind her, and leaned her hands on the sink. She looked at her reflection in the mirror. The dark circles showed, despite the makeup she'd caked on that morning. She turned on the sink and wet her hands, then pressed them on the back of her neck and waited while the anxiety passed. When she felt steady again, she returned to her father's study.

"Well then," he said, when she sat back down. "Would you

like to stay for dinner? Your mother is out for the night with some girlfriends, so it's just you and me."

A wave of surprise and unexpected pleasure washed through Veronica. "That would be wonderful," she said.

Veronica took a sip of her chardonnay and glanced at Robert, who appeared to be dozing off in his seat. She put her own seat back and closed her eyes. Before long, she felt herself getting sleepy, and had just started to doze off when a sudden thought sizzled through her brain and jolted her awake. During her last visit, she had left her purse unattended in her father's study when she made an excuse to leave the room to get some air. Generally, she wouldn't even be considering this. But now, she couldn't help but wonder. Could he have been the one to plant the tracker?

20

*R*obert had this dream many times before. He was running through the forest in France. Someone was behind him. He didn't dare turn, or the person might gain on him. When he came to a clearing in the woods, their cottage sat at the other side of a small creek. He started to cross the water, but the creek suddenly turned into a raging river, and when he looked for the house, it was gone. When someone put a hand on his arm, he jumped.

"Sorry if I woke you. Did you want some dinner?" asked Veronica.

"Uh, yes, thank you," he said, pulling out his tray table so the flight attendant could set down his meal. He took the band out of his hair and gathered the stray ends, then wound it back onto his ponytail.

"You haven't received flak from the agency for wearing your hair long?" asked Veronica as she cut a piece of chicken with a plastic knife.

Robert chuckled. "At times, but I'm good at what I do, so they leave me alone."

96

Veronica picked up her roll and tore off a piece. "Being good at what you do does come with some perks."

"Like getting more and more difficult assignments?"

Veronica nodded and took a drink of water. "Yes, but I guess you could say that is a double-edged sword."

"Indeed." He cut into his chicken and mused, "I sometimes wonder where I end and the work begins."

Veronica wiped her mouth with a napkin and appeared thoughtful. "I hadn't thought of it like that, but I would agree I've experienced the same."

When they'd finished their meals and their trays had been cleared, the flight attendant came on the intercom with an announcement about upcoming turbulent weather. The remainder of the flight was indeed a bumpy ride. When they arrived at Toulouse-Blagnac Airport the following day, Robert looked forward to getting off the plane. He had slept fitfully during the flight.

As they headed away from the airport, Robert eased the car into bustling traffic, car horns honking around him every few seconds.

"Where are we headed?" Veronica asked.

"Just outside of Lourdes. In the foothills of the Pyrenees."

"Do you really think your sister is holed up there?"

Robert shrugged. He preferred not to talk more about it, and Veronica seemed to get the hint. Things were rarely easy with his sister, who had caused her share of trouble over the years. She had seemed to settle down and let go of her demons once she'd left Shivers and had Sassy. He'd been glad when that happened because he knew from experience that dragging demons around with you was always at your own expense. He glanced over at Veronica, who was admiring the open fields. The view of wildflowers on this late spring evening soon became breathtaking. Veronica seemed the most at ease since he'd met her. He was surprised at the camaraderie that appeared to have developed between them.

TWO HOURS LATER, they passed through the small, southwestern town of Lourdes, France, famous for its healing waters. He drove through an area of breathtaking architecture, then headed southwest into the forest. Under the shroud of trees, the light quickly dimmed, so Robert switched on his headlights. It was quiet here in the woods. When they came to the turnoff he knew well, he made a right.

The cottage sat deep in the country, bathed in a kind of pearly radiance from light filtering through the canopy of trees. Vines of ivy blanketed the stone front.

Robert shut off the engine, and his stomach dropped. No sign of a car, and the place looked empty. "We should use caution going in," he said.

"Give me my gun, and I'll back you up," Veronica said, holding out her hand.

Robert pulled her beretta out of his bag and handed it to her, then he got out of the car, and she followed. At the front door, he tried the doorknob. Locked. He took out his key and slid it in, opening the door as quietly as possible. Standing on the threshold, he listened intently.

Veronica peered in a front window. "I don't see anything," she whispered.

Robert opened the door, gun drawn. Nothing in the small front room with its green velvet-like couches and coffee table heaped with magazines. "I'll check the bedrooms, if you can check the kitchen and mudroom," he said.

His heart hammering in his chest at what he might see, he headed down the short hallway and pushed the first door to the right open with his foot. No one. The peach coverlet was still perfectly smoothed and tucked in as if he never left. No one in the bathroom, or the room where Sassy stayed when she visited. He went to the kitchen to find Veronica peering into the trashcan. "There's a phone in here," she said.

Robert went over and picked the phone out of the trash, holding it up. "This looks to be Fiona's." He glanced around the room. "Nothing else has been moved or disturbed."

"It appears she doesn't want to be tracked," said Veronica. "Has she done this sort of thing before?"

Robert pulled out a chair from the kitchen table and sat down. "Yes, but not since Sassy was born. I thought she'd given up on all of this."

"All of what?"

"Looking for our mother."

21

"*I* didn't realize your mother was missing," said Veronica, watching as Robert rubbed his finger over a burn mark on the table. She waited for him to reply.

"Fiona did this with one of her blasted cigarettes," he commented. "Whatever she could do to push the limits, she did." He sat up in the chair and glanced out the window, then answered her question. "My mother isn't missing. She's dead. A fact that Fiona still hasn't been able to accept." He stood and went over to the refrigerator and pulled it open, inspecting the contents. "I'll make us some dinner."

Robert clearly didn't wish to speak about his sister or mother, so Veronica decided to drop it. Besides, she was hungry. "That would be nice," she said. "What can I do?"

He reached into a basket for a couple of potatoes that he washed in the sink, then peeled and began dicing on a cutting board. "I'll let you do the dishes."

Veronica laughed. "Let me. Interesting choice of words."

Robert turned and gave her a smile, then said. "You don't laugh much. It's nice when you do."

Veronica felt her cheeks warming. "I guess I don't have that much to laugh about."

Robert finished dicing, then pulled a frying pan from the bottom of the cupboard and fired up the gas range. He drizzled oil into the pan, then threw in the potatoes and stirred with a wooden spoon as they sizzled and sparked. "There's always something to laugh about," he said, opening the refrigerator and reaching in for a bowl of eggs.

Veronica thought about his comment. "Maybe it was the way I grew up. All was serious at my house."

"Your father appears quite stern."

"He wasn't stern so much as serious."

"And your mother?"

Veronica lifted the saltshaker in front of her and examined the grains. She sighed. "My mother in many ways is an enigma. Everything with her is about what is customary. From years under the watchful eyes of diplomats, I suppose."

"A rather staid way to grow up."

Veronica set the saltshaker back down. "That's one way to put it."

By now, Robert had finished the egg dish and set a plate in front of her. "I have wine. A red from Burgundy."

"That would be lovely," said Veronica.

After dinner, Robert headed toward the back door. "I'm going to go look at the stars, if you'd like to come."

Veronica watched after Robert and suddenly felt nervous. She took a few deep breaths, then got up from the table and ventured outside to find him staring up at the sky. When she saw his handsome profile, she just stood there transfixed, unable to speak.

With Veronica next to him in the moonlight, Robert felt that her energy had changed, become softer, yielding, shy even.

"You must be worried about your sister," she said, suddenly.

"I am, but that's not what I was thinking about." He looked at Veronica as she stood motionless. "I was thinking," he continued, "how lovely you look in the moonlight."

"The other night in the kitchen..." Veronica trailed off.

Robert waited.

"I didn't want you to stop kissing me," she said.

At her words, Robert reached for Veronica and pulled her to him. When their lips met, the fire that had been smoldering inside of him exploded into a bonfire. After several long, serious kisses, he breathed into her ear, "Do you want to take this to the bedroom?"

Veronica nodded, and Robert took her by the hand into the cottage, shutting the door behind them. He thought about picking her up and carrying her into the back room but didn't want to do anything that might make her reconsider. He would let her set the pace.

Inside the small bedroom, Veronica turned to look into his eyes, then slipped her hands beneath his shirt and smoothed them over his chest, before lifting the shirt over his head. Her skin felt hot against his. She silently unzipped his jeans to discover he wore no underwear, and let his pants drop to the floor. When she took him in her hands, a shudder passed through him, and he groaned.

She stroked him for a few minutes, then he took her hands and smiled. "My turn," he said, stepping out of his pants, then leaning down to kiss her, his tongue intertwined with hers, their mouths unwilling to leave one another's. After a while, he unbuttoned her blouse, sucked and kissed at the soft part of her neck, nibbled her left earlobe. He then ran his tongue along the top edge of her black lace bra. In a throaty voice, he said, "Turn around."

Veronica's breath caught at the force of Robert's words. She turned, and he undid the hooks of her bra. Then he cupped her breasts in both hands and pulled her even closer, his penis hard against her backside. Her breathing became shallow, matched with his as he helped her shimmy out of her pants and slipped his hands into her panties. He then took them off, his hands so large and warm, she wanted to cry at the intensity of her feelings.

"It's my turn," she said, in a tremulous voice and turned, smiling mischievously in the dim room. She didn't want Robert to stop touching her but put her hands on his chest and pushed him toward the bed. He sat on the edge while she remained standing, then suddenly, he grabbed her and pulled her up into the middle of the bed and flipped her onto her back. He looked deeply into her eyes, one hand on the side of her face and the other grasping her hip as he entered her. For the first time in her life, Veronica felt tears threaten when he claimed her. His lovemaking seemed as if it was more than physical or transactional—that it mattered somehow.

When they finished and lay in each other's arms, she felt an unexplained deep emotion overtake her. So great was the feeling that when Robert asked her a few minutes later if she was awake, she nodded her head rather than answer. That way he wouldn't see her face wet with tears.

22

*R*obert woke suddenly. Veronica was crying out, her arms thrashing around. He grabbed one arm when it came close to striking him and said forcefully, "Veronica, wake up."

She opened her eyes and gave him a quizzical look.

"You must have been having a nightmare."

Veronica ran a hand across her face.

"Do you want to tell me about it?"

"Why are you so concerned?" she snapped, then her eyes softened. "I'm sorry. I know you mean well."

"I'm going to get us some water. No pressure." Robert went to the kitchen to fill two glasses and came back to see Veronica leaning against the headboard. She accepted a glass and took several large swallows. He got back into bed and waited for her to speak.

"I'm not used to whatever this is," she said. She tucked the sheet around her body, encasing her breasts, then shook her hair back away from her face.

Robert smiled. "Confiding in someone?"

She nodded and took another sip of water. "I didn't have

any siblings to whisper secrets to. To be honest, I'm not sure how this is done."

Robert reached out and stroked her cheek. "You just start."

Veronica let out a long sigh. "I was on a mission a month ago. The target, Joseph Wenderson, had holed himself up in land outside of Provo, Utah. He had been calling himself the Messiah to a cult of devoted followers, but the CIA believed it to be a smokescreen for a terrorist cell. They discovered he had ties to an Afghani rebel group and believed there were several foreign nationals there posing as cult members. I was sent in to determine if the terrorists were there and if the threat was valid."

She rolled the cold glass across one cheek. "I've had other assignments with immoral, depraved men, so I wasn't too concerned, until I met him. Something about the way he pulled people into his orbit, especially young women, was unsettling. He wasn't pleasant to look at, really. But he was a practiced charmer who spewed B. S. out disguised as gospel. He plied impressionable young women with what he called offerings in the form of bracelets, necklaces, combs to wear in their hair, cheap things that sparkled and caught their eye. When I arrived, he had already impregnated at least three young women in the cult. He was always careful to wait until they were eighteen."

"Where was Horatio in all of this?"

"He was posing as a new convert, like I was, just on the male end of things." She took a deep breath. "Wenderson had these ceremonies where he..."

"Take your time," said Robert. He laid a hand on her shoulder.

"He would 'anoint' the women while everyone watched." She looked at him knowingly. "Everything short of inter-course meant to impregnate, which he called a baptismal ceremony. The women were drugged first with what he called 'holy tea' to make them more compliant. Everyone was encouraged to chant during the whole thing. It was horrifying to watch him undress those girls, paw over their young bodies, and expose himself. Then he would take them into his private quarters to consummate the union."

"Bloody hell," said Robert almost to himself.

"This is all so sordid," she said. "You don't want to hear this."

"Whatever you want to share," Robert said.

"We'd been given strict orders. He was not to be harmed. We were just to gather intelligence and determine if the cult was in fact a terrorist cell. If it was, the FBI was going to come in and shut it down and apprehend Wenderson, and then the CIA would notify Interpol regarding the Afghani terrorists."

Veronica pushed her hair back and took another sip of water, then continued. "Wenderson had eyes everywhere in his compound. It wasn't easy to move around without being detected. That made it slow going in terms of gathering intelligence about a possible terrorist cell. On one occasion, I did find what looked to be bomb-making materials, but I was interrupted by one of his many guards and brought back to my post in the kitchen. Soon after, I was told that I was next up for the ceremony. I managed to let Horatio know, so he could check the compound during that time."

She set the water glass on the bedside table. "I was given the tea, but when no one was looking, I tipped it into a potted plant, then acted intoxicated during the ceremony. The plan had been for Horatio to come in and stop Wenderson when he brought me to his room but one of the men caught him snooping around and detained him. Wenderson was a big man, and strong. I had intended only to stop him with the paring knife I had stolen from the kitchen and sewn into a seam in the dress they made me wear, but when he ripped off the dress and threw me across the bed, his body like a giant, squirming slug on top of me, I thought about all the girls he had violated, and I knew he would do it again. My ripped dress lay at the foot of the bed. I twisted to it and grabbed the knife. I meant to threaten and scare him enough to let me go, when suddenly he pounced all his weight on me, and the blade ripped into his gut. I knew he would kill me if he survived, so I stabbed him in the heart. He bled out quickly. Horatio got the brunt of the blame for Wenderson's death for not backing me up. He did find evidence of a terrorist cell that night, though."

Robert turned off the bedside light and pulled Veronica to him. "The son of a bitch is dead now and can't ruin anyone else's life. Try to wipe it from your mind." He stroked her hair for some time as they lay there in silence. At one point, he felt her body become slack, and she fell asleep.

Veronica woke to sunlight filtering through the bedroom windows. Her back was nestled against Robert's chest. He was still asleep, his breathing steady and slow. She thought about the night before and felt lighter having confided in him. As if she could breathe easier.

From her vantage point, she saw through the bedroom window sunlight filtering down in golden shafts. She felt like she needed to feel its healing warmth and inhale the fresh air. Carefully, she slid out of Robert's embrace and eased from the bed, then walked across the hardwood floor. She quietly pulled open a bureau drawer and found a man's t-shirt that she let slide over her head and naked body. The fabric smelled faintly of cedar.

She stole out of the room and shut the door. In the kitchen, she found some teabags and filled the kettle with water. After lighting the gas range, she unlocked the back door and slipped outside to walk across the dewy grass, the sun warm on her shoulders. At the edge of the land was a field of wildflowers. The sweet smell of flowers filled the air. She stopped to watch a bee forage in a bright yellow flower. Then her eye caught a small forest on the other side of the meadow, and she headed that way. She wondered if Robert played here as a child. Did he run across the field and ripple of wildflowers to hide from his sister in the trees? When Veronica entered the forest, she noticed a hush amongst the trees, as if she'd entered another world. Then she heard trickling water and followed the sound until she came to a stream that wound its way toward a lake in the distance.

Robert climbed his way out of sleep to a high-pitched sound that he soon recognized as the teakettle. When it didn't stop, he slipped out of bed and pulled on a pair of shorts, noticing that a bureau drawer had been opened. In the kitchen, he expected to see Veronica, but she was nowhere in sight. He turned off the range, then filled the two cups sitting on the counter with piping hot water and added teabags. Seeing that the door was unlocked, he stepped out into the morning sunshine and glanced around, finally spotting Veronica in the woods beyond the meadow.

"You're up," she said when he was a few yards away.

"The teakettle."

"I'm sorry. I thought I'd go right back in but it's so peaceful. Did you play out here as a boy? Are there fish in the lake?"

Robert must have gotten an odd look on his face, because Veronica said, "Did I say something?"

"It's a long story," he answered, dismissively.

Veronica put her hands on her hips. "That's not fair. It's your turn to tell me something. Why the long face about the lake?"

"I'll tell you over a cup of tea," said Robert, then turned and headed back to the cottage.

23

*R*obert took a sip of his tea and set the cup back down on the kitchen table. "Our mother was complicated, according to my Uncle Campo, her brother. Fiona takes after her, it seems."

So that was the deeper connection Veronica had sensed between the two men. "I didn't know he was your uncle," she said.

Robert raised his eyebrows. "I would have thought Horatio gave you that information."

"He just said there was a connection between you both. You said your mother died?"

"When I was an infant. She drowned. Fiona was six."

"Where? Not in the lake here?"

Robert ran his hands through his hair, which hung loose around his shoulders. "Yes, here. My mother had a boat she took out onto the lake. Sometimes she'd take Fiona with her. The only trouble was that my mother couldn't swim. She said the fish would save her if she ever fell in." Robert stopped talking and added more cream to his tea, then took a sip. "As I mentioned, my mother was high strung. My uncle also thinks she may have had postpartum depression from my birth. One day when it was storming and I was napping, she went out on the boat all alone and it capsized. My uncle arrived at the cottage a few hours later to find Fiona hysterical and me crying for a feeding."

"That's awful," said Veronica. "How difficult for your sister, especially. But if your mother died on the lake that day, why does Fiona keep looking for her?"

"After my mother passed, the locals started an urban legend, saying that every time there was a storm, they saw a woman walking around the lake. For years, Fiona would come here hoping to see her, I suspect."

"So, your uncle stepped in to raise you. What about your father?"

"My mother never divulged who he was, not even to my uncle. Quite a sordid mess, as you can see. It likely makes your staid upbringing look decidedly better."

Veronica reached out and gently stroked the top of Robert's hand. "I'm so sorry. It must have been difficult growing up not knowing your parents."

"I don't have any memories of them. It's hard to miss someone you never knew." He sighed. "Fiona, though, remembers bits and pieces about our mother. The memories have driven her in some strange way. But I thought she'd finally gotten herself together and given up on all that. It still makes no sense to me that she would leave Sassy. That's something she hasn't ever done before."

"Maybe she realized what a mistake she made and is on her way back to California right now," said Veronica.

Robert frowned. "That's possible, I suppose."

Veronica felt a sense of disappointment wash through her. She finished her tea. "Well, then, you best get back to California to see if Fiona has returned. Maybe you can point me in the direction of a car rental place. I can drive to Spain."

Surprise filled Robert's eyes. "If my sister is on her way to California, she'll contact me when she arrives about Sassy's whereabouts. There's not much I can do now. And we had a deal to help one another. I can go with you to Spain."

Veronica opened her mouth, then closed it and just nodded.

"You were going to say something?"

Veronica looked away, then back at Robert. "Thank you."

"That wasn't hard to say, was it?"

Veronica laughed. "No."

"If we head out now, we can get there by early evening."

"I just want to check my phone messages on the computer," she said. "See if Horatio has sent anything." After Veronica logged in, she saw only messages from her mother, asking if she was okay and saying she had something to tell her. Veronica couldn't reply, knowing they had to be monitoring her mother's email. She thought about calling, but that too would likely be overheard. She felt terrible for keeping her mother in the dark. She closed the computer and got ready to leave.

A few minutes later, Veronica watched the cottage recede through the car window and felt a twinge of sadness. This had been an interlude she would remember for some time.

As Robert drove south toward Spain, a comfortable silence settled in the car. They drove straight through, making good time, stopping just once for petrol. When they arrived in Valencia, dusk had fallen in the port city, and the city's lights twinkled. Robert rolled down the window and welcomed in the fresh ocean breeze.

"Have you been here before?" he asked.

"No. Where are we headed?"

"I say we check into a hotel to give us a base of operations. Then we can strategize our next move."

Veronica watched Robert expertly navigate the crowded streets, hitting the brakes when cars in front of them ground to a halt. After a time, they came to Hotel Balneario Las Arenas. He pulled in front and stopped the car. "I'll go get our room." Before Veronica could respond, he had hopped out of the car and made his way through the giant glass doors.

As she waited, Veronica thought about the last few days' many events. She was used to an ever-changing landscape with the work, but it wasn't ever so personal. That excited and scared her all at the same time. When Robert strode toward the car with a smile on his face, Veronica couldn't help but return his smile.

He got in and handed her a keycard, then started up the engine. "We have an ocean view," he said as he maneuvered toward the hotel's underground parking garage.

Veronica grasped the card in her hand, a warm feeling rushing through her. "That's lovely, but I don't know that it's necessary."

"On the contrary." Robert drove into a parking spot. "I've been to this hotel before. When I saw the photo of your father and Sokolov, something jogged my memory. I think they were standing in a spot that overlooks the water at this hotel."

Robert's phone buzzed in his pocket. He took it out and checked the screen. "Bloody hell."

"What is it?"

"A woman's body was found washed up onshore not far from the hotel earlier this afternoon. Looks like it may be Anya Sokolov."

24

*V*eronica was shocked but wasn't going to let the news deter her from her mission. There was too much at stake. "Everyone leaves a trace," she said. "We'll find something." She put her hand on the car door handle. "Shall we?"

When they got to the room, she waited while Robert slipped the keycard in the lock. Veronica felt a shiver of pleasure at the prospect of spending another night with him. He pushed the door open and flipped on the lights to illuminate a large room with a king-sized bed and a kitchenette. The bathroom door was open, and she could see a large bathtub and gleaming marble sink. Veronica walked over to the sliding glass door and pulled it open. Humid air swept in, and she could hear the ocean.

"The room is quite nice," she said, turning to see that Robert still stood in the doorway. He held his phone in his hand, his face pale.

"What is it?" she asked.

Robert didn't speak, so she went to peer at his phone.

There was an image of a woman bound and gagged, and a message underneath. *1 million, or she dies.*

"Is that Fiona?"

He nodded.

Veronica put her hand on his arm. "What are you going to do?"

"I don't have a million dollars." He looked at the photo of his sister again, eyes filled with anguish.

"Should you call your headquarters?"

"And say what?"

"It's okay. It's okay. We'll figure something out."

Robert scrolled through the rest of the text. "It just says they'll be in touch."

He walked over and sat down on the edge of the bed, and Veronica sat down next to him. "The most I could cobble together would be $200 thousand, and that could take a week," he said. "Shivers, Sassy's father, has the funds, but that's a conversation Fiona would have to have, and I'd likely spend days trying to get through his army to talk to him."

"I have the money," Veronica blurted, surprising herself. She felt sick at what she had just seen on Robert's phone.

Robert looked at her, shock registering on his face. "You're joking."

"I wouldn't joke about a million dollars. Do you think Fiona could get the money reimbursed by Shivers once we get her?"

"I think she probably could, but I can't let you do that." He reached for her hand. "We don't even know where she is." He was breathing fast. His face red.

"Her cellphone was in France, so it's likely she's nearby."

Robert nodded and looked at his phone again, his brow furrowing.

"We'll do everything we can, and more, to get her out of this," said Veronica.

Robert couldn't believe Veronica was offering to pay for his sister's release. Was this the same woman who'd planned to hold him at gunpoint just three days ago? She got up and opened her laptop, setting it on a nearby table. Then she pulled out a chair and began typing. "I need to make a transfer. If I start work on it now, we should have the money by morning." She looked up and raised an eyebrow. "This is your turn to say thank you."

He went over and took Veronica's arm, then lifted her to him. They kissed, and then he buried his face in the crook of her neck and softly wept. Veronica froze. She didn't move or speak, instead let him struggle with both the fear for his sister and relief over the money. She put her arms tighter around him, unused to dealing with another person's emotions, including her own. She realized he loved Sassy, but he obviously loved his sister a great deal, too. What she wouldn't give for that kind of love. Something she had never known.

"I'm sorry," said Robert, wiping his face on his sleeve. "I keep thinking how devastated Sassy would be to lose her mother."

"You, also," she said. "Don't apologize. I wish there was someone who would shed tears over me." She laughed lightly and sat down at the desk. "Let me transfer the money." She entered information into the computer, and after a few more keystrokes, smiled up at him. "All done."

Robert pulled out a second chair and sat down next to her. He placed his head in his hands, then took a deep breath. "There's no way to thank you enough," he said.

"You asked the other day why we do this work," Veronica said.

Robert looked into her eyes. "I remember."

"This is why. So that we're ready and able to help when those we love are in danger. That day has come for you, and for me. Your sister doesn't deserve this, and neither does my father."

"Speaking of your father," said Robert, holding up a finger, "I was thinking on the drive here how his predicament could in some way be linked to the threat against your secretary of defense." He opened his phone and pulled up a file he'd gotten from the data intelligence unit before he had to make a mad dash for Sassy. He began reading the information out loud. Veronica picked up a notepad and began taking notes of the contents of intercepted conversations, much of which was quite cryptic.

Once Robert had finished relaying all the information an hour later, she got up and began pacing, stopping several times at the table to consult her notes. Robert could almost feel her thinking. Finally, she sat back down and began tapping the pen on the table.

"There's a cadence to the conversation, and a progression." She handed him the notepad, pointing a lacquered fingernail at a string of numbers. "I think these are coordinates." She flipped the page. "And 1400. I believe that is the time of the planned assassination."

"You are good," said Robert. "It would have taken me days to figure that out."

"I doubt days," said Veronica. "Besides, we still need to determine the who and the date. I'll leave that to you."

Robert slid the computer in front of himself and called up the MI6 database. "I noticed in various conversations just now a repeated identification phrase. It's being used by a Russian pseudo military faction disguised as Americans that

MI6 has been tracking," said Robert. "It could be they are behind the assassination plan. Quite brilliant, really. Create chaos and confusion as your government looks for unrest from within, then strike from without."

"That is something." Veronica stood and stretched her back. "But we need more answers. Like their motive, and what my father has to do with all of this."

Robert's phone pinged just then, and he checked the screen. "The woman they found in the water was Sokolov. They found another body, as well. A man."

"Now I'm grateful my father is in jail in the States," she said. "Have they identified the man?"

Robert slowly nodded. "CIA agent Horatio Soledad."

25

*V*eronica's hand went to the base of her throat. Her face bore a mix of disbelief and worry. "That explains why I haven't been hearing from Horatio."

"How long did you know him?" Robert asked.

"More than a decade. We did quite a bit of sparring over the years, but he was a good agent. And he did have my back on many occasions. We shared one especially dangerous assignment designed to gather intelligence on an international arms dealer in Belize. Horatio intercepted a hit man one night that had been put on my trail. If it wasn't for him, I don't think I'd be standing here right now."

"Seems you've been involved in pretty dangerous undertakings."

"Our occupation isn't for the faint of heart." She gave him a steady look. "Tomorrow is just a couple more fights for the two of us to win."

"Why don't we get some sleep?" suggested Robert and gave her back a quick rub with one hand. "We can tackle all of this in the morning."

Veronica stood. "I'd like to sleep for a thousand years."

Robert smiled as he watched her gather her things and go into the bathroom. Then he made a call to Helga.

"Robbie, so glad you rang."

"Is Sassy, okay?"

"She's fine. It's your uncle."

"Tell me." Robert chewed his bottom lip.

"He's left. Earlier this afternoon."

"How? He doesn't have a vehicle."

"I was preparing his tea when some military chap by the name of Monte came by in a jeep and swooped him up. Said they had business to attend to. I warned your uncle that his wound wasn't healed yet, but you know him."

"Did they say where they were going?"

"No. Just that there were some things to handle. How about you?"

"I'm getting closer to Fiona. Hopefully, by this time tomorrow I'll have her."

"Oh, Robbie, that would be wonderful," said Helga. "You're still with the woman you left with?"

"Yes, and all is working out well."

Helga was silent, then replied, "I'm glad you and the woman are a good fit. Just take care, Robbie."

"I'll be in touch as soon as I have Fiona," Robert promised.

"We talked," said Helga. "Campo and I."

"A fruitful conversation, I hope."

"Let's just say, we're getting there. Some things were explained, on both of our parts. It's good you brought him here."

Robert took a deep breath. "You know how I feel about what happened. You were only doing what you thought was right for Fiona."

"And now so are you," said Helga. "Thank you, Robbie. I know we all want her back safe with Sassy."

Robert smiled. "I'll let you get back to my niece. I've got to get some sleep."

Helga chuckled. "You get some sleep, Robbie." And then the phone clicked off.

Veronica's head spun as she stepped out of the shower. Horatio and Sokolov dead. Her father incarcerated. She towel dried, racking her brain for next steps, but none came. Maybe Robert was right. She needed rest.

When Veronica walked out of the bathroom, Robert was laying on the bed in his clothing. She saw the look on his face, his eyes taking in her half-clad body loosely wrapped in the bath towel, her legs bare, wet hair splayed across her breasts. They both had a lot on the line tomorrow, she thought, and needed to clock at least five or six hours of sleep. Not being on their game, unaware of dangers around them, could get them killed. She could feel her heart beating and wanted to drop the towel and go over to him. Instead, she padded to the end of the bed and slipped off his shoes, unfurled his socks and slipped them inside. He looked up at her. "Let's sleep," she said softly, wrapping the towel a little tighter. Robert nodded and yawned, then slid out of bed to strip naked before climbing back in. When he turned on his side, she flicked off the bedside lamp and let the towel drop before climbing in naked.

"You sure you don't want to..." his voice trailed off, showing the need for sleep. She pressed her body against his warm back and kissed his shoulder. "Tomorrow," she promised and knew he was probably smiling. It wasn't long before she felt his body slacken and give way to sleep. As she listened to his slow and steady breathing, she realized that for the first time in her life, she felt safe. The thought made her feel so calm and peaceful that she soon felt herself slipping into dreamland, as well.

At some point in the night, Veronica awoke to Robert's long muscular body beside her. He must have gotten up and showered, because he was still unclothed, and he smelled of soap. He pressed his erection up against her and whispered, "Perhaps I can show you how grateful I am for taking off my shoes?"

Veronica turned to him. "That would be very nice of you."

When Veronica awoke in the morning, the room was swathed in dim light, the heavy curtains still drawn. She glanced at the clock, 6 am, and heard tapping on the other side of the room. She turned in the bed to see Robert hunched over the computer.

"I believe I've figured out the when." Robert wore briefs and nothing else. A warm heat washed through her once again.

She sat up in bed. "When?"

"Today."

"That gives us just eight hours to warn someone at the Department of Defense. How I wish I could just call my father." Then she had a thought. "Do you think he knew about the assassination plans and that's how he ended up framed?"

"I'm beginning to think that's a distinct possibility. We may have reinforcements coming, including someone we can inform of the assassination plans. My uncle Campo and a US military chap. If I can get ahold of them."

"Who's the military man?"

"First name is Monte. That's all I know."

"Arroyo?"

"Do you know him?"

"I believe my father does. You said, if you can find them."

"I've got a call out for them. Helga told me they left the cabin several hours ago." His phone pinged, and he checked it, his brow furrowing.

"What is it?" Veronica asked.

"The kidnappers want to trade Fiona for the money today."

26

*R*obert got up from the computer and began pacing. Then he went over to the sink and started filling the coffee pot with water.

Veronica watched him for a moment, then sat down at the computer and pulled up her banking information. "Good news," she said when her bank balance popped up. "The money is in my account. We can wire transfer into the kidnappers' account, but not until we get Fiona. Have they given you a location yet?"

"No."

"Keeping you on your toes," she said, tapping a fingernail on the edge of the desk. "Any word from your uncle?"

"Nothing there, either."

Veronica got up from the computer and went to the closet where she'd hung her clothing and pulled out dark blue slacks and a white silk blouse. "I'm going to get ready while we think of next steps." She grabbed her makeup bag and headed to the bathroom.

Robert considered their next move. They weren't doing any good from here. It was time for some action. His heart raced at the prospect of something having happened to his sister. He'd been able to push the worry into the recesses of his mind, but now just hours from hopefully retrieving her, he worried even more that she could already be dead. He heard the sink turn on in the bathroom. Robert poured himself a cup of coffee and added some creamer, then took several quick swallows. He set the cup down just as a loud knocking sounded at the door. He went to the peephole and checked. "Blast it all," he muttered as he opened the door a crack and peered out, "Yes?"

"*Hola, señor,*" said the man, who flashed him a badge and quickly closed the cover. "I am with *la policía.* We understand you are here with a female guest?"

"I am," said Robert. "And you're disrupting us."

The man, who had a bushy mustache and slicked back hair, cleared his throat. "*Lo siento, señor,* but we are looking for a fugitive." He pulled out a photo of Veronica. "Do you recognize this woman?"

Robert looked closely at the photo, then shook his head. "I can't say I do."

"This isn't the woman you are with?"

"The woman I am with, no, definitely not." Robert cleared his throat. "Now, if you don't mind, I'm quite busy."

The man stretched his neck to get a look inside the room. Seeing nothing, he bowed his head slightly and said, "Excuse me for bothering you."

Robert shut the hotel door and bolted it. As he did so, Veronica emerged from the bathroom fully dressed.

"Who was that?" she asked.

"A police officer, who had a photo of you with your former hair color."

"That's odd that the local police would be looking for me," said Veronica.

"I was thinking the same thing," said Robert. "I think it's time we get out of here. We can wait for the kidnappers to contact us from a safer location."

Veronica glanced at him, a thoughtful look in her eyes. "Why don't you leave first, and I'll wait twenty minutes and follow."

When Robert left a few minutes later, Veronica finished gathering her things, and put her laptop in the safe. She realized she'd left her cellphone in the bathroom and went in to retrieve it. Just as she was doing that, she heard a key in the lock and thought Robert had forgotten something. When she went back into the room to see why he had returned, she came face-to-face with Horatio. Veronica stepped back and gasped.

"What are you doing? Sleeping with the enemy?" he asked, a sneer on his face.

Veronica's eyes went to her purse, where she had put her gun. "I could be asking you the same thing," she said.

"Don't bother trying for your gun. I've got it." He grabbed her, wrapping his hands around her forearm, making her wince in pain.

"Seems you layer one lie on top of another," she said. "What do you want, Horatio?"

"You'll soon find out."

Robert waited in the park near the hotel for Veronica. When twenty minutes came and went, he checked his phone again. No texts. He sat on a bench where he could watch for her, but after what he thought a reasonable amount of time, decided to go back to the room to check on her. The walk did him good, gave him time to clear his head. When he entered the room a few minutes later, he saw Veronica's purse on the table. He opened it and checked inside. Her cellphone wasn't in there, nor her gun. He glanced around the room. Nothing to give him a clue as to if there might have been trouble. There was only one way to find out. He went down to the lobby and strode up to the reception desk.

"Excuse me miss, but I'd like to see your manager."

The hotel clerk's eyes opened wide at his urgent tone. "Is there something I can help you with, *señor?*"

"I need to speak to your manager immediately."

She made a quick call, and a man in a black suit came out from a back room. "May I help you?"

"Could we speak in private?" Robert asked him.

"Of course," the man said, gesturing for Robert to step into the back room with him.

When they were in an office, the manager gestured to a chair in front of a desk. "Have a seat."

Robert remained standing. "I believe a woman has been abducted from the hotel."

"*Señor*, we must call *la policía*," the man cried, reaching for his phone.

"That's not necessary," said Robert. "I'm with a security agency. I just need to see the footage from the hallway in front of my room for the last half hour."

The man hesitated.

"If your patrons find out that guests are going missing," Robert said in a low tone, "that would not be good for business."

"Let's take a look at the video footage." The man finally decided. "Come with me." They walked down a short hallway, then into a small room filled with surveillance screens. A hotel employee sat in front of them.

"Felix, this gentleman would like to see the footage in front of his room over the last few minutes." He addressed Robert. "Your room number?"

"Six-seven-six," said Robert.

Felix punched on the keyboard in front of him and pulled one of the screens toward them. "How long would you like me to go back?"

"Thirty minutes," said Robert, watching as Felix backed up the footage until a man and Veronica exited the room. He could only see their backs, but the man held her close. Veronica didn't appear to be leaving willingly. "Go back to when the man entered," he instructed. Soon, he watched as a man came up to the doorway. He kept his head down, then a family exited the room across the way, causing him to glance up for a moment. "Freeze that, please," said Robert. He studied the man's face, then checked his phone. If Robert wasn't mistaken, Horatio Soledad had arisen from the dead.

27

"*Where* are you taking me?" Veronica asked.

She sat in the back of a sedan with one of Horatio's men, a gun trained on her. Horatio was driving.

He cussed as a bus stopped short in front of them, and he slammed on the brakes. The movement took the man guarding her by surprise, and Veronica grabbed the gun, twisting it in one quick movement from his grasp. Before he knew what happened, the tables had turned. "Don't be stupid enough to try anything," Veronica said. "I'll blow your head off just to entertain myself."

Horatio glanced back and snickered, then began driving again. "Forget about it, Valencia, or should I call you V.V., like your pal, Shayla?"

A cold sense of apprehension swept through Veronica at the mention of her friend's name. "What about Shayla?"

"I have a man ready to slice her throat back in Arlington should you refuse to do as I instruct. If you doubt me, look at this." He threw a cellphone into the back seat. Veronica picked it up with one hand and glanced at the screen, stifling a gasp. Shayla, bound and gagged in her apartment.

"What do you want, Horatio?" Veronica's throat felt so tight she could barely breathe.

"Justice. Think of this as a chance to redeem yourself."

Veronica kept the gun trained on Horatio's man while her mind whirled. "Is this about the last case?"

Horatio turned onto a narrow side street and slowed the car. He glanced in the rearview mirror, his eyes flashing venom at her. "That, and much more."

More? Veronica thought. She couldn't imagine what he was talking about. But one thing was for certain, Horatio was looking for vindication.

They pulled up next to a building with a fire escape. There was a black door just beneath it with a sign that read, *privada.*

Horatio turned. "You can hand the gun back to my man, now. Unless you want me to give the okay to end your friend's life. A little slice from ear to ear? Up to you."

Veronica handed the gun back while Horatio got out of the driver's side and came around to the back, pulling the door open and tying a handkerchief that smelled of his cologne around her eyes. Then he yanked her out of the car while she heard what sounded like a heavy door being opened. Cool air rushed at her as she was pulled inside. They walked for a short distance, then another door was opened, and she was pushed through its passageway. The door slammed shut behind her, and the sound of it being bolted echoed in the dark space. She tore off the blindfold, her eyes meeting with darkness. She could sense someone near her. Pulling out her cellphone, which she had hidden in her bra, she hit the light, then shined it around the space, stopping to stare in shock at what she saw. There in the corner of the room sitting on the floor against the wall was Anya Sokolov.

Robert had precious little to go on, except for Veronica being with Horatio. Anxiety threaded through him at what Horatio planned to do with her. He headed back to the room to decide on his next move.

When he pushed the hotel room door open a few minutes later and rushed in, he stopped short. There stood his uncle.

"I know that look. What's gone wrong?" Campo asked.

"Everything," said Robert.

"No word on your sister?"

"I'm trying my hardest to get to her, but the cowards want a ransom." His phone buzzed, and he read a new text from the kidnappers. "They want me to bring the money in ninety minutes. They'll be giving me the location soon."

Campo's eyebrows shot up. "I was hoping this was just one of her disappearing acts. How much?"

"One million," said Robert, scanning the room for Veronica's computer.

"Where do you plan on getting that kind of money that quickly?"

Robert spotted the cabinet door to the safe slightly ajar. He went over and kneeled, putting in the code they had given them at check-in. He breathed a sigh of relief to see that Veronica had the foresight to stash her computer in there. He stood and handed it to his uncle. "This belongs to the CIA operative I left the cabin with. She was set to lend me the funds for Fiona."

His uncle eyed the computer, shock on his face. "You traveled here with Valencia? Where is she?"

"Missing."

Campo looked at Robert with incredulity.

"I believe one of her associates wants her dead," Robert added. "I saw him take her from the room on the security footage."

Campo sat down at the table. "This is quite a mess. Do you have any idea where Valencia is now?"

"I might have a line on that," said a man, who walked into the room at that moment. "You must be Robert. I'm Monte Arroyo." He wore jeans and a t-shirt, but Robert could tell he was military, with his close-cropped hair and the way he stood, legs apart, back straight. He jutted out a hand to shake Robert's.

Campo cleared his throat. "Monte is here to collect Ms. Valencia."

"Our intel says that she and Valencia senior have been selling secrets to the Russian government for the past decade," said Monte.

Robert felt a surge of anger pass through him, but he kept his tone level. "My intel says otherwise. In fact, I would bet my life on it."

Monte's gaze fell on the unmade bed, then he looked back at Robert. "I don't mean to speak out of turn here, but take it from me. Women have a way of warping a man's perception."

"My perception is crystal clear," said Robert. "I'm assuming you know where she is, which is why you're here. What you don't know is that your secretary of defense is set to be assassinated today. I have that information, and I'm willing to trade it for Veronica's whereabouts."

Monte's face turned to stone. "Look, Harroway, she's a wanted fugitive for treason. I can't just hand over her whereabouts."

Robert advanced toward him. "You can, and you will. Or how will you explain to your superiors that you let the secretary of defense take a hail of bullets?"

Monte glanced at Campo, then back to Robert. "Give me credible information, and I'll give you her whereabouts, but she's still going to face the treason charge. You need to bring her to me."

"Just as soon as we have proof of her innocence."

Monte considered for a moment, then reached out his hand and they shook.

While Monte called the Secret Service about the threat to the secretary of defense, Robert asked Campo, "Can you access Veronica's funds for the ransom?"

"It's not looking good, I'm afraid. The files are triple encrypted. I think our best bet is to retrieve her as quickly as possible, so she can access them."

Robert checked his watch. He had a little more than sixty minutes until he was to meet the kidnappers with the money.

"I'll go with you," his uncle said, standing, then gasped as he clutched his side.

"What is it? Your wound?" asked Robert.

"Just give me a moment."

"There's no time. Stay here and keep Veronica's computer safe. We'll need it to access the ransom. They're going to text me her location soon. If I can't make it back in time, you can meet me."

As he headed out, fear burned in Robert's brain at what could happen to both his sister and Veronica. He could not lose either of them. Unfamiliar words tumbled from his tongue as he prayed to get to both women in time. He knew the probability of accomplishing a rescue grew more improbable by the second. Both their faces floated before him, and he made a pact to use everything in his power to free them.

hen Robert arrived at the address Monte had given him, he decided to approach from the back. He came upon a door that read *privada*. It was locked. Above his head, he saw a fire escape. He quietly pulled himself up and began making his way to the second floor where he saw an open window.

"You're Anya Sokolov," said Veronica to the woman in the room with her.

Anya nodded slowly, then recognition dawned in her eyes. "You're Veronica."

Veronica waited for Anya to continue speaking, but she didn't. "How do you know me?" she said finally. "And how do you know my father?"

The woman brushed a lock of blond hair from her forehead but didn't reply.

"They are saying my father has been feeding you US secrets. But I know better. Are you blackmailing him?"

The woman's eyes held much emotion. Veronica could see curiosity, bewilderment, pain, but still she failed to respond.

"My father is a good man. He would never betray his country." Veronica edged her way closer to Anya. "Whatever it is you are telling them, you must take it back. They are going to try my father for treason. If you are his mistress, tell me."

"I am not his mistress," said Anya quietly. "I am his daughter."

Veronica thought her ears must be deceiving her. "What did you say?" she stammered.

"We're half-sisters, you and I." Anya hesitated. "Forgive me. I would not have wanted to tell you this way."

Veronica felt dizzy with confusion. "But how?" she managed to say.

"Our father and my mother," the woman stated simply. "They met during the end of the Cold War. He was in Russia when Gorbachev resigned. It was a weekend affair, but my mother became pregnant."

Veronica did the math. She would have been six at the time, and as she recalled, Gorbachev gave his resignation speech on Christmas Day 1991. She remembered her father not being home for the holidays that year.

"My mother told me my father was a Russian soldier," Anya continued, "that he had died during military service."

By now, Veronica believed her. "Why did you come forth? I'm assuming you went looking for your, our father?"

"My mother died ten years ago, and I found my birth certificate. No name of a Russian soldier on the document."

"My father's name?"

She shook her head. "It was blank. But I found photos of our father in her things and was struck at how much I looked like him. That got me to thinking, so I contacted him and we met when he visited Russia. He knew the moment he laid eyes on me."

"But how do you know for sure?"

"We took a DNA test," she said.

Veronica studied Anya's face. She had her father's eyes and nose. A sister.

"How is he?" Anya asked her.

"I haven't seen him since before he was arrested." Veronica glanced at the door. "Why is Horatio holding us?"

Anya licked her lips, which appeared cracked. "I'm not sure. He grabbed me a couple of days ago, and I've been here since. You work with him, don't you?"

"Yes, I'm ashamed to say." Veronica stood up and began walking around the room. She pulled her cellphone from her bra. No reception.

Robert paused in the bottom floor stairwell, listening for any sounds. He pushed the door open slowly and looked into the hallway. Empty. As he emerged, he kept his hand on his gun in the back of his pants. A door flew open and an armed man came out, aiming at him as Robert pulled his gun. But just as quickly, a voice behind him said, "Put your weapon down, Harroway, and kick it toward my man. Now."

Robert did as instructed, then slowly turned to face a man with a thin black mustache. "You must be Soledad," he said. "I've come for Veronica."

The man smirked. "Valencia does tend to turn men's heads. But beneath that lovely breast of hers beats a stone-cold heart." He nodded toward his guard. "Put him in the room at the end of the hall."

When the light switched on and Horatio entered, Veronica sprang to her feet. "What is it you want? Are you such a little man that you must keep two women captives to feel powerful? I'm afraid that will never help."

Horatio's eyes hardened, and he sneered. "Always such a big mouth, and you don't think before you speak." He looked from Anya to Veronica and grinned. "Are you two getting to know one another?"

"If you mean that Anya is my sister. She told me. No point in threatening to hold that over me."

Horatio kept his gaze on Veronica. "You haven't considered the consequences of this? Your father and a Russian woman, lovers during the Cold War. Him raising two families for years. Living a double life."

Veronica glanced at Anya.

"Oh, our little Russian spy didn't tell you that part? Daddy was there for all of the important moments in her development."

"Is this true?" Veronica didn't know who to believe anymore.

"Don't listen to him, Veronica. Like I told you, I didn't meet our father until ten years ago."

Veronica felt a hot surge of anger course through her at the thought of her father meeting a secret daughter for the last decade. All his talk of duty and honor. She turned to Horatio. "What does this have to do with you?"

"You may recall that my father and yours crossed paths years ago when they both worked here at the Spanish Embassy?"

When Veronica didn't reply, he continued. "My father should have gotten the position at the White House that resulted in your father's steady climb to power."

"That's it? You resent me for what I've had?" said Veronica.

"For such a good agent, you are abysmal when it comes to personal matters. The top-rated Ivy League school your parents afforded you. The house in Georgetown. The vacation home in upper New York. Those should have been mine. Instead, I had to claw my way up, all because my father was passed over for a traitor. He died six months ago in an inferior care facility, because my family couldn't afford any better."

"How is killing me and Anya supposed to remedy this?"

Horatio laughed. "Kill you? I have captured a suspected traitor and her spy sister. I'm bringing you both back to the United States where you'll stand trial for treason with your cheating father. Anya here is proof of the cheating."

"How do you expect to take a Russian citizen to the US for this farce?"

"Your dear sister is a dual citizen. And she's witness to your and your father's crimes, and likely connected. So, this will be a win-win for all parties, except yours."

"All because you couldn't go to Princeton. Ruining people's lives with a childish temper tantrum?"

"I am just doing my job. Speaking of which, good work with Harroway. He played the hero and came after you, so we have him now, too. I'm sure my sending the assassin after you helped you play the damsel in distress."

Veronica felt her breath catch. "Robert has nothing to do with this."

"Dear Veronica, have you forgotten your assignment so quickly? You were sent out to detain Harroway, so we could get information from him. We're doing just that. I have to say it will be a shame to lose your considerable talents at reeling in men, but I'm sure I can find another female operative to train."

Veronica shuddered to think what Horatio might do to Robert. "If you let me see him," she said, "I can get the information you need. We've developed a rapport."

Horatio laughed. "From what I saw, you've developed more than a rapport." He glanced away for a moment, then turned to her again. "Five minutes. You get what we want, then I won't have to send in my man with the cattle prod."

Horatio turned and rapped on the door. A guard swung it open, and he motioned for Veronica to leave the room. "Ladies first."

"You mean prisoners first," she shot back. In the hallway, Horatio took hold of her arm and led her to a closed door. A guard stood out front.

"Get me information about his uncle's current assignment."

"He's not going to give that up."

Horatio motioned for the guard to open the door. "Oh, I think he will. If he ever wants to see his sister alive again."

Veronica swung to face him. "So, you have her? What about the ransom?"

"Just something to smoke Harroway out when he extracted the funds. But I have to say, I was surprised you were the one who got the money. It was a stroke of luck. More proof of how you and your father have been taking money from the Russians all these years. Go in, now. Your Brit is waiting."

Veronica went into the room and her heart skipped a beat to see Robert sitting chained to a metal table.

When Horatio slammed the door shut, Veronica rushed to Robert, kneeling next to his chair. "Are you okay?"

He smiled. "Now that I'm seeing you."

Veronica's heart softened at the tenderness in his eyes. "I'm sorry about this. About Horatio," she said.

"None of this is your fault. Tell me, what does the madman want?"

"To offer me up as a traitor. And to get information on your uncle's latest assignment. I told him you would never give up Campo, but it's him who has Fiona."

"Dammit," Robert said, hitting a fist on the table. "So, it was a ploy. To get me to cooperate."

"Looks like we're at his mercy," said Veronica, feeling a thread of fear work its way up her spine.

"Maybe not," said Robert. "Campo and Monte came to the hotel. It was Monte who gave me your location. They're on to Soledad. We just need to get an SOS out to them."

Veronica pulled her phone out again. Still no bars. She composed a brief mayday text, then walked around the room until, in a flash of reception, it sent.

The door swung open then and Horatio stood on the threshold. "Tell me you have the information I want."

"Not until you release my sister," said Robert.

"Well, then, we have a problem," said Horatio, who crossed his arms over his chest.

Veronica advanced toward him. "Where the hell is she?" She grabbed his arms.

Horatio's eyes turned red with fury. "As usual, Valencia, you have no idea who's in charge." He motioned to raise his arms to loosen her grip, but she dug her nails into his flesh as hard as she could. He reacted to the pain, which gave her a split-second to knee him in the groin. As he involuntarily doubled over in pain, she yanked his gun from his hands and leveled it at his face.

There was a knock on the door. "Everything okay in there, boss?"

"Say everything is fine," Veronica hissed. "Or I shoot. Now."

"All's fine," Horatio called out as she reached into his pocket and extracted a key ring, then tossed it to Robert, who unlocked the chains and freed himself from the table.

"Where is Fiona?" said Veronica in a low voice, the gun aimed between his eyes.

"You're not going to kill me," said Horatio.

"But I will shoot you. Your kneecaps, maybe? Under your belt? I'll get creative."

He considered her words, then looked to Robert and back again to her. "I sold her."

"I don't believe you."

"Have you seen Fiona? The sultans love her type."

Veronica studied Horatio's eyes as she held the gun steady. "Where is she now?"

"Most likely about to leave the port for the Far East."

"So now you're adding human trafficking to your list of transgressions? Give me your phone. Enter the password first."

He handed it to her and she scanned the texts. "It looks like he's telling the truth."

Horatio began to protest as Robert pulled him by his shirt collar over to the table and chained him there. "This isn't going to work, you know."

"Shut up," said Robert. "I'm done listening to you."

Just then there was a commotion outside the room, and the door burst open. Monte Arroyo and two men charged in. "Veronica Valencia, you're under arrest for treason against the United States government."

29

*V*eronica raised her arms as the men came toward her. When they started to handcuff her, she informed them, "This is the phone of CIA agent Horatio Soledad. It has evidence that he has sold a woman and is keeping two women hostages—one down the hall and another in the States. He is also responsible for framing me and my father for treason."

Monte took the phone from Veronica's grasp and checked out some of the text messages. He looked at Robert, then back at the phone. "Your uncle indicated that something along these lines could be occurring."

"I don't belong in handcuffs," cried Horatio. "I have an operation to run."

"The only thing you're going to be running is your mouth," said Monte. "Tell me where Fiona Cartwright is."

"She's about to be taken out of the country," said Veronica. "Please, have your men stop the boat before they get to international waters. And he has someone holding FBI agent Shayla Foster hostage in her home in Arlington."

Monte radioed in an order to have the vessel stopped and

searched, and then placed a call for the military police to go to Shayla's. When he finished, he said, "I want to talk with you Ms. Valencia, and Soledad here."

"The US military has no jurisdiction over this," said Horatio. "When my superiors find out what you've done, Arroyo, you'll be finished."

"My orders came from higher than that. I'd stop protesting if I were you."

Monte's satellite phone sounded then. He answered and listened for a moment. Then he turned to Robert. "Your sister has been rescued."

"Thank god," said Robert. He threw his head back and exhaled a long breath.

"I can have one of my men take you to her," said Monte. When Robert looked at Veronica, he added, "I need to keep her for questioning."

Though Robert was relieved to know his sister was okay, he hesitated to leave Veronica.

She reached out and touched his arm. "Go to your sister. She is probably terrified."

"Okay." He looked indecisive for a moment. "I'll contact you after I get her."

As Robert walked toward the door, he looked back at Veronica. She gave him an encouraging smile, then looked away.

At the port a few minutes later, he climbed out of the car and slammed the door shut. Large expensive boats and yachts bobbed on the ripples of water along the dock. Robert took a deep breath of the salt air and looked up at the clear, blue sky overhead. A car door opened across the lot, and Fiona stepped out. Her face lit up, and she came running toward him, her long, silken blond hair whipping in the wind. She flung herself into his arms. "Robbie," she cried, "I knew you'd find me."

He squeezed her hard, kissing her hair, then her cheek. "I'm so sorry this happened to you." He swallowed hard and held her, not wanting to let go.

"I'm still in one piece," she laughed through her tears.

"You're safe now. I've got you," he soothed, rubbing her back.

"How is Sassy? Is she alright?" Fiona asked, pulling out of his embrace and searching his eyes.

"Sassy's fine. She is a brave, strong girl just like her mother."

Fiona nodded her head and smiled.

BACK AT THE HOTEL ROOM, Campo jumped up from the table as they came through the door. "Fiona! You are a sight for these old eyes!"

The two embraced, then Campo winced.

"What happened?" asked Fiona.

"A minor mishap," he said. "I'm fine. I'm more concerned about you."

Fiona laughed. "Only you and Robbie think something like getting bit by a rattlesnake is a minor mishap. I can't wait to hear your story. I'm starved and in great need of a shower, but I'm okay." She then looked from Robert to Campo. "I'd love to talk to Sassy."

"It's a bit late to wake her," said Robert. "She's in California."

"Who is watching her?" Then realization filled her eyes. "She's with Helga?"

"Yes, and she's fine," said Campo. "I was there myself for a bit recovering."

Fiona looked at her uncle. "You've made up with her?"

"We're working our way toward amends, yes."

Campo and Fiona stared at one another, until Campo approached Fiona and gently rested his hands on the sides of her arms. "It's time to let what Helga did go, Fiona. She only had your best interest at heart. I understand that now."

"She had me committed."

"Why do you think I hadn't spoken to her for years? But I wasn't the one to find you walking barefoot around the lake in the middle of winter looking for your mother and talking gibberish. She didn't know what else to do."

Fiona sighed. "I know you're right. I'm going to need some time. I'm just grateful that Sassy is safe, and that I'm alive." She looked around. "Whose room are we in?"

"It's mine," said Robert.

She pointed to the closet. "Have you been wearing women's dresses?"

"I'll catch you up on everything later. I have to go finish business now. You're in good hands until I get back."

Fiona looked concerned.

"Trust me?"

His sister hesitated, then nodded and embraced Robert again.

As Veronica answered Monte's questions, she couldn't

help but think about Robert. She hoped Fiona was safely out of the kidnapper's clutches and reunited with her brother by now.

"So," said Monte, "your father had a child with a Russian woman."

"I knew nothing about this until a few hours ago."

"Do you think your mother knew?"

Veronica thought for a moment. "She could have. My parents have always been a united front, so I wouldn't be surprised."

Monte rolled the pencil he'd been taking notes with between his fingers. "According to your mother, who I spoke with at great length yesterday, she did know about Anya."

Veronica shifted in her chair.

"I'll be honest with you, Ms. Valencia. There is still a lot of evidence piled against you and your father, but I've a mind to believe you. Soledad has been playing it fast and loose for a long time. And he's in boiling water now for human trafficking and keeping an FBI agent hostage. But I can't let you go just yet. I'm going to have to take you back to the States and keep you in custody pending further investigation. I'm sure you understand. We've got a military jet cued up at a nearby airfield." He waved over one of his men.

"What about Robert?" asked Veronica as the man took her arm.

"He's free to go back to his life," Monte said.

When Robert parked Campo's rental car in front of the building where he'd left Veronica, he was encouraged to see the door still open. He went inside, but his heart sank to hear the quiet. An American military man walked out from one of the rooms and asked, "Can I help you?"

"I was here earlier," he said. "Has everyone left?"

The man nodded. "We're collecting evidence from the scene, but yes, everyone involved has vacated the premises."

"There was a woman with Lieutenant General Arroyo. Veronica Valencia. Do you know where she is?"

"She was taken to the airfield nearby for transport to the United States."

"Has the flight left?"

"I'm not sure. Excuse me, I have to get back to things."

Just then Robert heard the thunder of a plane taking off. As he stepped outside onto the gravel lot, he saw a military jet lifting into the sky overhead.

30

*W*hen they arrived in Washington, Veronica was held and questioned for three days. The grilling was exhausting. They kept asking the same questions, each time approaching them from a different angle. The interrogations went on for hours, whether she was hungry, tired, or angry and fed up. She found herself repeating the same thing over and over. She knew what they were doing. Trying to wear her down to see if her story would change, but it didn't. There were times she couldn't help but smile to herself. Several of the investigators were simpletons, easy to see through. When it came right down to it, she was smarter than they were. If she had anything to hide, which she didn't, they would never be able to trip her up.

While they held her, she had given permission for them to scour her electronic communications, and her financials. The million dollars she'd taken out for Fiona had raised red flags, until she showed that she'd gotten the money as an inheritance from her grandmother when she passed.

At first, at night as she lay in her cell, she thought of Robert. Memories of their short time together would fill her head, and a lump would form in her throat. She remembered his sure, slow smile, and how it felt to have his strong arms around her. But she decided it was best to push the memories away and concentrate on getting out of custody. One thing she knew for sure, if she didn't cooperate and make her story believable, it wouldn't go well for her.

On the second night, her mother came to visit. Veronica had been eating her dinner when she heard doors clang and sure footsteps. When her mother wound her hands around the bars of her cell, Veronica set down her fork and walked over to her.

"Veronica." Her mother's voice was full of rare emotion. "Are you okay?"

"As okay as I can be, given the circumstances." Veronica noted the worry lines around her mother's eyes. She hated the distress she always seemed to cause her and felt certain all her mother wanted was a respectable daughter with a boring nine-to-five job.

Her mother reached out for her hands, and Veronica took them. "I'll get you the best lawyer, if necessary," she assured her.

Veronica took a deep breath, then asked, "How is father faring?"

"It looks like he will come out of this, but not unscathed. I'm not sure he'll be able to return to the DOD."

Veronica wasn't sure how to ask the next question. "Mother, did you know about Anya?"

Her mother frowned and looked through the bars past Veronica's shoulder before she replied. "Yes, your father told me soon after she contacted him when her mother died. It was a very bitter pill to swallow at first. You can imagine. I guess I loved him enough to work it out."

Veronica pulled her hands away. "And you didn't tell me? All of father's talk of duty and honor."

"That's exactly why I didn't tell you. What good would that have done you? You've idolized your father since you were a child. I wasn't about to take that from you. Besides, it was a lapse in judgment on his part. He was remorseful and never strayed again."

Suddenly, the pieces came together for Veronica. "He gave Anya money, didn't he? That's why the government flagged him as a traitor. They thought he was paying for secrets."

"The payments have compounded matters, yes, but they are ironing that out now that Anya has come forward." Her mother paused. "My conscious forced me to care what happened to the girl, to Anya. I let your father take care of that and we never discussed it. All your father and I ever wanted for you was the best, V. Someday when you meet a man you care for and have children of your own, you'll understand."

Robert flashed across Veronica's mind and a yearning like she'd never felt before swept through her. She wished she could see him, touch him, hear him say that everything would be okay.

"It's going to take me some time, Mother," she said. "But I'll do my best to get there."

ON THE THIRD AFTERNOON, they released Veronica, completely exonerated. Her father was set to also be let go soon. Veronica didn't need to report to her new supervisor at the agency until tomorrow. So today, she planned on going to her parent's house and showering and climbing into bed.

She was about to flag a taxi when someone touched her arm. She knew before she turned who it was. "I can take you wherever you want to go," Robert said quietly as she turned to face him.

The tears Veronica had been holding back since she'd left him in Spain poured down her face now. When he wrapped his arms around her, she felt an overwhelming sense of joy and let herself get lost in his embrace.

"I'm so sorry I couldn't be here with you," he murmured in her ear as she cried. "But I'm here now."

Veronica pulled back and attempted to wipe away the tears. "I didn't think I'd ever see you again," she said between sobs.

Robert gave her an odd look. "You couldn't keep me away. Not with the way I feel about you."

Veronica held her breath, unable to respond.

"As in, I love you. I want to be with you, Veronica."

Robert watched Veronica's face as his proclamation set in, hoping he hadn't made a bloody fool of himself. She looked concerned.

"I love you, too," she said, her eyes warming at his words. "What do we do?"

Robert laughed. "Do? I vote for taking you back to my hotel room and ravishing you."

Veronica laughed. "I meant about your job and mine?"

He hushed her with a kiss, then said, "We can figure that out. Who knows, maybe I'll retire and write spy novels."

Veronica looked dubious. "You'd do that?"

"I'd do anything to be with you. Now let's stop standing

in the street. People are starting to gawk. My suite is in the best hotel in the city. Let's take advantage of it."

"I love the best hotels," said Veronica as Robert took her hand and flagged down a taxi.

EPILOGUE

 eronica's and Robert's stories are complete, but Hans Wagner's is just beginning...

HANS WAGNER CHECKED one last patient chart and signed in all the appropriate places. It had been a long, twelve-hour shift, and he was beat to the bone. Visions of the hot shower and hours of sleep he'd soon be enjoying made him smile. He walked down the hall of Mercy General and handed the chart to the nurse on duty, a petite brunette, whose name escaped him now.

"Mr. Beck's chart," he said, checking out her name badge, "Nurse Martin. Keep an eye on his blood pressure. The Chlorthalidone should start kicking in soon."

The nurse smiled as she took the chart. "Yes, Dr. Wagner. Are you off now?"

"I am. Dr. Phelps is on call, but he should be in soon. I wish you a quiet night."

"The same to you."

Hans went to the men's changing room and opened his

locker, then pulled off his scrubs. He was just going home, but he liked the ritual of changing clothing. It shifted the energy from work to personal. Other doctors would trail out in their scrubs after a shift unless they had other plans. They liked to joke that Hans was anal-retentive. There might be some truth to that, he admitted, but he had a feeling his patients appreciated their doctor being organized. And patients were his top priority. Feeling refreshed in jeans and a t-shirt, Hans grabbed his bag and shut his locker, then headed out of the hospital.

Though it was just after midnight, the temperature still hovered around eighty degrees. Los Angeles in August had a way of doing that. Hans approached his Lexus, but blinked several times when he saw someone sitting in the passenger seat. A woman. He pulled his cellphone out of his pocket, ready to dial 911, while he approached cautiously. "What are you doing in my car?" he asked, staying back several feet.

The woman opened the door, revealing a gun in her hand, directed at him.

"Your services are needed, Dr. Wagner," said the woman, who had flaming red hair and wore sunglasses. "Get in the car. Now."

Hans backed up. "I'm not going anywhere with you."

"Your mother, Gretchen, enjoyed a meal of macaroni and cheese earlier tonight at her assisted living facility in Sherman Oaks. It would be a shame if she didn't wake up in the morning."

An icy sliver of fear ran down Hans's spine. He put his cellphone back in his pocket and walked over to get into the driver's seat....

Find out what happens with Hans in *Discovered Obsession*.

A NOTE FOR YOU

Dear Reading Gem,

Thanks for spending time with me, Veronica and Robert! While each of the books in the Discovered Truth Series can be read as a standalone, it's fun to experience the progression and get to know the characters. The series progresses as minor characters introduced in each book become main characters in subsequent books. It's exciting to see what they'll do next!

The Discovered Truth series features complex, gutsy women and equally complicated, charismatic men who find themselves immersed in dangerous and intriguing modern-day challenges, such as human trafficking, drug smuggling, organ theft, national security threats, and identity theft. When the heroine and hero meet, worlds collide and sparks fly, kindling unforgettable romance and intrigue.

If you like the series, please leave a review or just stars on any book review platform. Your opinion matters and is incredibly powerful.

Thanks again and talk soon!

STAY ENLIGHTENED

Thanks for reading! Let's stay in touch. I post insider information, and sneak peeks of upcoming books on my website at https://www.juliebawdendavis.com/fiction. You can also email me at Julie@JulieBawdenDavis.com, find me on Facebook, and follow me on Amazon.

Even better, join my weekly VIP Reading Gems newsletter here. When signing up, you get a free copy of *Discovered Beginnings*, the prequel novella to the series. There are also lots of giveaways and contests!

Escape to Unforgettable Romance and Intrigue...

BOOKS IN THE DISCOVERED TRUTH SERIES

Discovered Beginnings:
(FREE at https://www.juliebawdendavis.com/fiction)
Discovered Secrets
Discovered Memories
Discovered Indiscretions
Discovered Liaisons
Discovered Betrayal
Discovered Denial
Discovered Distractions
Discovered Deception
Discovered Lies
Discovered Vengeance
Discovered Redemption
Discovered Obsession
Discovered Transgressions
Discovered Suspicion
Discovered Escape
Discovered Promises
Discovered Cover-up

Box Sets

The Discovered Truth Series Box Set Books 1-4
The Discovered Truth Series Box Set Books 5-8
The Discovered Truth Series Box Set Books 9-12
The Discovered Truth Series Box Set Books 13-16